Praise for Books
By Rob Pierce

"Rob Pierce is one of the more imaginative literary voices in our new emerging era of noir."

—James Grady, author of
Six Days of the Condor

"Rob Pierce is urban noir's high priest from the mean streets."

—Joe Clifford, author of the
Jay Porter Series

"A detailed and empathetic portrait of a personal struggle with demons we may not all face directly, but which always lurk beneath our carefully calculated covers. Pierce rips off that lid and exposes the common darkness of all our souls, whether we want to admit it or not."

—Will Viharo, author of the
Vic Valentine, Private Eye Series

"Dustin is one of the most memorable characters to emerge from this genre since Richard Stark's Parker. Flawlessly executed, *Uncle Dust* should move to the top of your list if you are a fan of hard crime/noir fiction."

—Greg Barth, author of the Selena Series

D1594183

"Dark as hell and exceptionally engrossing. Read this one, and be glad you don't have an Uncle Dust."

—Nick Mamatas, author of *I Am Providence*

"One of the best noir and crime novels of the past five years. Pierce has done a masterful job of playing high drama and low stakes where the heart of the story isn't about the big heist, or the big show down, or the fight scenes, but of the complicated nature of being a criminal, and a creature of violence, but not a simple caricature. A fantastic read for fans of cynical, dark, and yet hopeful tales of people who pay for their mistakes and have to keep the change."

—Jason Ridler, author of *Hex-Rated*

"Rob Pierce is a new talent that cuts deep into the underbelly of society and rips the guts and heart out of his protagonist."

—Lou Boxer, Noircon

"The story and dialogue in *Uncle Dust* capture much of the circumstance of prison life in all its squalid glory. Made me wish I'd done time with tough guy Dustin. I thoroughly enjoyed our criminal hero's mind as he observed the world, and himself, through a cynical thief's lens. And I think you will too."

—Joe Loya, author of *The Man Who Outgrew His Prison Cell: Confessions of a Bank Robber*

WITH THE
RIGHT ENEMIES

OTHER TITLES BY ROB PIERCE

Uncle Dust
The Things I Love Will Kill Me Yet
Vern in the Heat

ROB PIERCE

WITH THE
RIGHT ENEMIES

All Due Respect
An imprint of Down & Out Books
3959 Van Dyke Rd, Ste. 265
Lutz, FL 33558
www.DownAndOutBooks.com

The characters and events in this book are fictitious. Any similarity to
real persons, living or dead, is coincidental and not intended by the
author.

Edited by Chris Black and Chris Rhatigan
Cover design by JT Lindroos

ISBN: 1-948235-23-4
ISBN-13: 978-1-948235-23-5

For those I haven't always stood by—sorry, sometimes a heart in the right place ain't enough. And some of us ain't got as much heart as we once thought.

We lose our innocence,
We lose our very souls
—Paul Weller,
"Tales from the Riverbank"

ACT 1

Vollmer stood in an alley, only thirteen but big for his age. He lived on the street, had to stay alive somehow, thought of jobs to pull. A short kid came running in, long dark hair flying, took the turn into the alley sharp and pressed his back against the wall. Vollmer was right next to him, figured cops or worse were coming, did the same.

There were sounds a street over, people running, no sirens. A couple minutes of that and they both exhaled, laughed at each other for doing the same thing.

"We laugh that loud," Vollmer said, bent forward from laughter, "they best be gone."

"They gone." The kid smiled big. "I fucking hope."

Both boys laughed again. They were boys and everything was a joke.

"Hey, Vollmer." It was a couple years since they met in the alley, but Chilly was still the same kid with the long straight hair and a grin that didn't always make sense. Happy way too much.

Vollmer knew who it was before he turned his head. He looked back and Chilly ran down the sidewalk to join him. It was evening and the sidewalk was crowded, but Chilly was skinny and agile, maneuvered through with minimal contact.

Vollmer grinned as Chilly caught up. "I woulda bumped a couple those motherfuckers outta my way."

Chilly raised his eyebrows and his grin broadened like the thought never occurred to him. Vollmer figured not a lot of thoughts did, but he was good for a few laughs.

"I know a couple girls," Chilly said. That was his idea of a greeting. Vollmer was okay with it. "Can you get us some blow?"

Soon as Chilly said the first line, Vollmer saw something like the second one coming. Chilly always had good news, if...

"I had blow," Vollmer said, "I'd be with a girl already."

"Yeah, well, I done the girl part for you. A gram and everyone's happy."

"A gram? How many fucking girls you get?"

"Two," Chilly said. "Plus there's two of us, that's only a few lines each."

"I'll go half a gram," Vollmer said. "I get my dick sucked, I don't need any fucking coke."

Chilly laughed like he'd already done a couple lines. "I dunno. Half a gram for three ain't a lotta lines."

"Get a sharper blade," Vollmer said. "Cut that shit thin."

Chilly was okay when there weren't girls or drugs involved, like a kid brother who wasn't that bright. Vollmer liked him, but he wasn't like him. They hung out, drank beer, smoked cigarettes and weed, told stories about stupid shit they saw on the street. It was a relief to talk to someone who lived casual like that, but Vollmer also felt he had to protect the kid, like Chilly didn't see things the way Vollmer saw them. Like Vollmer saw the world, but it wasn't Chilly's world. Thing is, it's the world. And it'll kill you whether it's yours or not.

Vollmer's early years were ugly. He was glad to be done with them and out on his own, but big for a teenager ain't the same as big on the street. This was a good place to get fucked if you weren't careful. Vollmer got his ass kicked a few times his first couple years out here but that was all.

There were women available of course, and he was a teenager, but he wouldn't settle for most of that. Back alley bitches and some homeless pretty girls, but they were always too fucked up to stick with, wanted some goddamn dream of world peace and weed, beads and patchouli.

Yula was this black chick, Ethiopian or something, young and smoking hot. She hooked for money so when they fucked he wore a rubber, but he lived on the street, whoever he fucked he wore a rubber. She had too much something in her eyes sometimes, residue of junk or whoring, and he knew from his short time on the street what that meant—she wasn't gonna get out of this, he'd better get it before it was gone. A shame, he really liked her, a funny girl when she wasn't too fucked up.

He paid her, her time was always money, but they'd get a room and he'd take it back while she slept. She never called him on it. Maybe she was too fucked up to know. Vollmer didn't buy it. Yula wasn't that far gone yet, she liked him but she had her pride. She got paid for what she did, then he got it back doing what he did. She never called him on it, never cut him for it. That meant she liked him a lot.

Vollmer had his pants back on, his Yula money freshly shoved into his pocket. She still lay naked under the sheet, her breath light in her sleep. His next step was to the door. But he always had time for leaving, didn't get many chances at this. He returned to the bed, dropped his pants on the floor, stepped out of them. The rubbers were on a little table next to the bed. He tore a packet open, slid under the sheet behind her.

One hand rubbed her belly while he moved up against her ass, legs against legs.

She stirred a little, spoke soft. "Baby."

That meant she didn't know who she was with. Not a problem, just the way she dealt with how her life was. Hell, Vollmer used that too, didn't always know the name of the woman he fucked, even if she told him when they met and he stayed sober the whole time. Maybe lovers need to know each other's names. Fuckers have a whole other set of cares.

He got her going, grabbed her shoulder and turned her on her back, forceful but she didn't resist.

"Oh, baby," Yula said, her eyes open and clear enough to know Vollmer, but it was good for her to never break the habit. Whores can't say the wrong man's name. A wife might lose a marriage that way, a whore might get beat to death. Not by Vollmer, though. She could call him anyone's name, so long as he got to look at her and fuck her. She was maybe fifteen and he was exactly, she was his birthday gift to himself. No one else he'd fucked looked like this. There weren't many girls who looked like this.

Large breasts, round ass, narrow, taut belly—Vollmer didn't know if that was an Ethiopian thing or if this girl was from another planet. Didn't matter; he got deep inside her and never wanted out.

She didn't make much noise while they fucked. Vollmer appreciated that. Wherever you are, don't call attention to yourself. He rolled off her, lay on his back, looked at the ceiling happy, turned his head to look at her again. Yula's eyes were closed, a smile on her thick lips. He wanted to kiss her but those were a whore's lips and anyway this was perfect.

The room didn't have a shower but it had a toilet and a sink. He walked in there and pulled the door shut, ran the water hard from the hot faucet—it was cold and he expected that, but it was worth a shot—and splashed it all over himself. The closest he'd get to a shower for a while. Vollmer took his time, got himself as clean as he could get these days.

He stepped back into the bedroom still dripping, spread his arms and legs and reached out. The stretch felt good, air against his skin. He stood there, limbs extended, showing off his lean muscularity, more comfortable naked than in his crappy clothes. Vollmer wasn't one of those street people with a shopping cart full of wardrobe and bullshit. He carried a sports bag with a couple spare pairs of T-shirts, jeans, and socks, washed them when he could, changed where he could. About time to go to a thrift shop and buy something new. New to him. He never stole clothes, that meant wasting time on shit that wasn't worth much.

"Hey," Yula said. "Whatta they call you?"

He looked at her, surprised. "Vollmer."

"Nah." Yula pressed both pillows against the wall and propped herself up. "I mean, your first name. What did your friends call you in school?"

A grin went up one side of Vollmer's face. "Friends?"

"Okay," her face changed, she got it, "the kids in school."

"Vollmer. Everyone calls me Vollmer."

Yula looked down, her hands did a church and steeple thing. She looked back up at him. "Okay. What did your parents call you?"

"Fuck them. I don't talk about them."

Yula blinked. "It's just you and me. What do I call you?"

Vollmer knew that was the opening part of him wanted. But he wasn't stupid, he knew what he was, knew what she was. "Call me Vollmer."

Vollmer had a man to meet. He'd work this deal then go back to the day-at-a-time income. Some fools mugged on the same street where they slept. Vollmer had bus money to get there, cab money to get back.

Williams was an old black dude, a wide motherfucker, strong but fat, maybe 400 pounds, like a defensive lineman gone to seed. Heavy in both size and power, a step up from the street level assholes Vollmer usually dealt with. The meet was out in the open, a downtown café with outdoor tables that would be impossible to bug. And the other tables at this joint? This warm day they were filled with men in jackets that covered guns.

Vollmer sized that up from the sidewalk, wasn't surprised, wasn't armed, and walked in. They had no reason to kill him and he wasn't going to give them one. He

6

was one man, fifteen years old, and these guys might have that many years killing people. And there were six of them. He walked into the courtyard and looked as unafraid as he could, stopped at the table where Williams sat with men on either side.

Vollmer looked the big man in the eye, tried to ignore the rest of the men in the courtyard. Most of them hadn't bothered with coffee cups. "I'm Vollmer."

Williams looked back with eyes that sized up and judged. "Sit."

Vollmer pulled out the cheap metal chair in front of him and sat down, waited for the big man to continue.

No one spoke for a minute. Williams looked down at him. "You got a deal or you gonna walk?"

"It's a simple deal," Vollmer said. "I'm gonna take down a card game on your turf. The game's private, not one of yours, and the guy who runs it don't matter."

"And you want help on the job." William's low voice had dropped an octave, down to a rumble like a threat.

Vollmer shook his head. "Just permission."

"That all?"

"And a job. You hear how smooth this goes, you gonna want me. You gonna want a piece of the next one."

Williams shook his head with a little smile. "I want a piece of this one."

"Put me on the payroll and you got it. Or I'm on my own and everything I get is mine."

"When's the job?"

"Friday."

"Not much time to get on this." Williams looked at the man to his left. He looked small next to Williams. Probably not next to anyone else. "You know who to call?"

The man nodded.

"Call him."

The man walked, made his call away from the table.

Vollmer clenched his fists on the table. "This guy gonna give me your answer?"

"We'll call you."

"Then I gotta give you my number." Vollmer stood. "Tell your guy I call. By Friday morning."

Williams smiled at Vollmer. Even that looked like a threat. "You want a coffee?"

"Nah," Vollmer said, "wish they sold beer. I'd take one a those."

Williams tilted his head at Vollmer, like he was focusing on his face. "You old enough to drink?"

Vollmer tilted his head to match. "Everyone's old enough for a beer."

Williams worked for Tenny. In this town, who didn't? That was the crowd Vollmer needed in with, and clipping a card game was no big deal. He'd broken into buildings before. This was some business place that let anyone in before five o'clock, just sign a name and the business you were visiting at the desk in the lobby. The game didn't start until eight; that meant a few boring hours in halls and bathrooms, boredom that would pay just fine.

Security was nowhere but in front, one guard and Vollmer was past him. A cleaning crew started around six, one Mexican each floor. Hell, maybe it was one Mexican for the whole building, all Vollmer saw was a pudgy guy with a portable radio on a cleaning cart. Songs cranked in Spanish signaled the cart's approach.

The card game was on the fourth floor and he'd get waved away if he showed up between seven-thirty and eight. The dick in that office set up early for the game and didn't like his room disturbed. Vollmer talked to the dick over beers in a dark bar one night—the joint served anyone, any age, cops this side of town had better things to do. The guy must like nasty thrills to drink in a place like that. Vollmer wasn't impressed.

He waited past eight, didn't want any late arrivals walking in behind him. This should really be a two-man job, but Vollmer didn't want to share the money. He waited until 8:30, pulled the ski mask over his head and tried the door. Locked. He knocked. "Hey, this the game?" Waited. A half minute, minute, two minutes.

Someone opened the door a couple inches. "Yeah?"

Vollmer pushed the door in hard, threw the short man behind it to the floor with the sweep of an arm. Vollmer's Browning 9 was out and he kicked the door shut behind him. Four guys in suits with ties loose or removed looked at him, their jaws down like he was God.

He looked at the guy on the floor. "With them."

The short man joined the table, struggled into the chair he must have just left.

"All the money on the table," Vollmer said. "One at a time." He pointed his pistol at a loose-tied man with a pencil mustache. "Pull anything but a wallet and you're dead."

Loose tie took a minute to get the wallet from his pants but he got it, pulled the bills and set them in front of him on the table.

"In the middle," Vollmer said. "Where the pot is. And straighten that stack for me."

Loose tie grabbed the money in the pot but it was all over the place, took forever to turn it into a stack.

"Stop," Vollmer said. "Y'all just stack your money on top of his. Next." He swung the Browning to the next man at the table.

The guy had his money out and stacked on the other guy's fast. Vollmer worked his way around the table. Everyone carried from the mid hundreds to the low thousands. If he got in with Williams from this, he could get an apartment. Too young to get it on paper, but the only paper Vollmer cared about was the green piling up on the table.

"Oh," Vollmer said, dropping all the money in a small grocery bag, "no one here's dumb enough to call the cops on this, right? Because I know who you are, and will come back and fucking kill you."

Knowing who they were was bullshit, but Vollmer could shoot them dead no problem. He'd never killed anyone, but if they were in his way he didn't see why not.

By the looks in their eyes, the guys at the table believed him more than they believed in cops.

Vollmer was 15 but looked 21, could get a room this side of town easy. The money stuffed in his front pockets had to be a few grand, he'd count it on a bed, maybe find Yula. If he didn't, he'd find someone else. He needed to celebrate. It was easier for Vollmer to get laid or get a gun than get a beer. That was alright. He preferred sex and pistols to drinking.

He didn't need to count the money yet—it filled his pockets and that meant there was plenty. He walked streets, saw everyone as prey. Middle of the night, prime time for whoring. Yula would make a lot more money with someone else. Or he could pay her more this time. Yula wouldn't go through his pockets, and she was the best fuck he knew.

He looked for her. Beautiful long legs in short skirts were abundant—not as beautiful as hers, of course, Yula was fucking perfect—a lot of other whores were too skinny above the waist and crack-mouthed—concave cheeks and missing teeth.

Vollmer knew the stretch Yula worked. She wasn't there. Other whores were consolation prizes, and he wasn't taking that tonight. Not this early anyway. There was plenty of time to pace the sidewalks and smoke, only it wasn't a great idea killing time on the street with a few grand on him. The neighborhood for hookers wasn't the same as the streets where you could sit in a late night café with a window view of the street. The rest of this block was ugly apartment buildings and duplexes, with a bar on the corner and a Mexican joint that closed hours ago on the next block, followed by more ugly apartments and another bar at the end of that block.

He'd find Yula soon or he'd leave this neighborhood and go to his usual room-for-a-night, hours to kill before he could sleep and nothing to do but exercise.

Vollmer strolled the street, maybe one last time, he didn't fucking know. A nice car pulled up at the next corner and stopped. The passenger door opened and legs got out. Vollmer knew those legs well.

He yelled from a block away. "Hey!"

Vollmer walked fast, reached her and talked in a hurry. "You're mine tonight. And it's a good night. You get double. I want everything you got."

She smiled. "You sayin' I ain't givin' you enough?"

"Sayin' I want everything."

They lay naked beside each other on top of the thin blanket. Vollmer kept a hand on Yula's hip and she ran a finger down his chest to his belly. They were young and in good shape, everything firm except where she was supposed to be soft. He tried to caress all those parts of her one after another, again and again.

"I get a real place soon."

"How'd you get the money?"

Vollmer smiled. "Same as always. Took it. Some guys got more to take."

Yula nodded like she knew. Vollmer didn't doubt it. He also didn't doubt Williams could set him up with a place. He didn't want to share a cut with anyone, but places he could rent on his own weren't places to keep money.

"You get a place," she said, "what do we get?"

"Same thing. Maybe a future. You want a future?"

"What I want…" Yula rolled out of bed naked, took two steps toward the bathroom and spun back, a view of all of her in one pirouette. "I want you." She turned again, took another step toward the bathroom and looked back over her shoulder. "And I'll be back for you. And I don't give a fuck about the money. I can always get money."

She stepped into the bathroom and Vollmer wondered. Maybe she didn't care about his money, only about hers. That mattered too, it showed she had pride. But she shouldn't have to make hers. He could take care of her soon.

She came out of the bathroom and approached the bed, each step off the balls of her feet, a slight grin on her face, like she was getting ready to pounce.

She stopped several feet away. "Remember that time that moppy head friend of yours come up, you and me heading off somewhere, and he wants you to run off and pull a job with him so he can impress some cunt with his money?"

"Yeah," Vollmer said. "Chilly's like that."

"Dick didn't even see me, so eager to get his own."

"Bet he pulled that job with someone."

"Or he pulled his own dick that night."

They both laughed and Yula took another step forward, on the balls of her feet again.

Vollmer eyed her, wanted her. "What'll you do," he asked, "when you don't have to whore?"

She stopped a foot from the bed, got on her knees and yanked the blanket off him. He was hard. She opened her mouth and went down.

Vollmer met Williams again, same outdoor café. "You got less guards this time. After that job, you trust me now?"

Williams shook his head slow. "I don't trust no one."

"Two guys. They your best?"

Williams nodded. "You got cocky since last time."

"I can find my own jobs. Do 'em, too. I need my own place."

"I know a guy. You bring my money?"

"You get yours, I keep mine. Where's this room?"

Williams widened his eyes, their whites in sickly contrast to the dark brown of his irises and skin, his pupils a black hole. "You got it in a envelope?"

"Got it in a pocket."

Williams laughed. "Jesus. How you gonna pass that without lookin' like the fuckin' crook you are?" He tipped his head back where his bodyguards sat, raised a hand. They both stood and stepped beside Williams. "Take this boy down the street, that fancy card shop, and buy an envelope big enough for my money. Then go to that bookstore, they got a bathroom in back, one of you goes in with him and puts my money in that envelope."

Vollmer stood, looked down at Williams. "They know how much is yours?"

"They was already in charge of countin' it. Won't take less. Won't take more. You all come back here, you get a name and number, you get a room."

"I ain't goin' in no toilet stall with these motherfuck-ers."

Williams lost his jolly demeanor, eyes practically shut but aimed straight through Vollmer. "Shoulda brought a fuckin' envelope."

House of Cards was a fancy joint for buying fancy cards, special occasions like that valentine you really liked or that wedding anniversary you didn't want to be the last. They sold fancy kinds of paper for formal invita-tions, had their own little print shop with letter press. And they had fucking normal envelopes, along with in-vitation sized ones, because your fancy shit had to get to your special people through the normal U.S. postal ser-vice. Vollmer didn't know what size envelope would hold a thousand dollars, but one of the bodyguards, a burly sonuvabitch who was obviously packing, walked straight to a small box of large envelopes and broke a twenty at the register. He pocketed the change, let the receipt fall in the bag.

They walked out to the sidewalk and the man who'd paid reached into the bag, opened the box and removed a single envelope, dropped it back in the bag. "One's good."

It was half a block to the bookstore and Vollmer didn't know what to expect in that toilet stall. He had another four thousand in his pockets on top of what he owed Williams. Not enough to kill him for but they still might try to take it from him. And this time he had a pistol, odds of someone dying were damn near guaranteed. They were not taking his money.

They strolled three wide, Vollmer in the middle, down the length of the bookstore. Where they didn't fit side by side, one bodyguard went in front of him, the other behind. Vollmer knew the other one a little. Stone. About his height, almost as fit, and mean as hell. Big hands too, so he favored big guns. Vollmer liked Stone, but not behind him, not right now.

Toward the back of the store the front bodyguard turned left. Vollmer followed, Stone behind him. They walked a narrow path until they turned left once more, into what was basically an indoor alley except it was clean and well lit—the way to the toilets. They walked past the women's room to the men's room several feet beyond.

They entered. The place reeked of shit. Two stalls, a handicapped one just past a normal one. Shoes and dropped belted pants were visible at the bottom of the handicapped stall. That was where the reek came from.

The front bodyguard stepped aside, faced the stalls from the row of three sinks. Vollmer turned his head and saw Stone still walking forward, toward the empty stall. Vollmer kept going. Stone followed him in, envelope in his hand. He shut the door, latched it, and opened the envelope wide.

Vollmer reached into his pocket. He'd folded a thousand dollars' worth of bills to keep them separate from his share, wedged them in. He could feel the folded bills, got his hand around them, brought his hand up. It stuck, couldn't get out of the pocket, too fucking tight. He tried again. Still no luck. Stone had a gun out. A Glock .50. Fucking huge. Nice.

Vollmer shook his head. "Not in here."

"You ain't got it?"

"I got it. Leave the envelope, I'll be out in a minute."

"I ain't fuckin' leavin' you."

There were grunts from the stall beside them. The smell in here was horrific. Vollmer coughed, covered his nose and mouth with one hand, whispered through his fist. "I won't leave the bathroom."

Stone shook his head, held an index finger straight up, twirled it in a circle, and pointed at the wall over the toilet.

Vollmer supposed that meant he'd be frisked. He shook his head. If he got frisked they'd take his pistol, probably keep it. He reached in his pocket again, kept his hand flat as he could, bent his fingers and grabbed the unfolded bills, pulled them out and started counting. He stopped when he reached a grand. A lot of the money was left. He handed the grand to Stone and pushed the rest back into his pocket.

Stone double-checked the count as he put the money in the envelope, then closed it with its metal clasp and stepped out of the stall. "Let's get outta this shithole."

* * *

They walked back to the café. Williams held his table like a king. "Got it?"

Stone nodded. "It's right."

Williams nodded. "Or the boy's suicidal." Williams brought a large hand down on one of Vollmer's. "Do what you want, I get a piece. Percent's on there." He nodded at a coaster near Vollmer's other hand. "And don't shit me on the take."

Vollmer shook his head. "Whole deal is, I get a nice place. Or I don't share."

"Take the coaster. Flip side's a number. Man named Dietz." Williams took his hand off Vollmer's, stood. "Get out."

Vollmer met Dietz in the building manager's office, a room with a desk and two tables that looked like they hadn't been dusted in a while.

"Sit," Dietz said.

Vollmer sat.

Across the desk, Dietz remained standing. A tall man in a black suit, he looked down at Vollmer. "Williams says you work for him and you need a place to stay. That right?"

Vollmer looked up. "Yeah."

"Yeah." Dietz ran a hand through his silver hair. He spoke with a harsh accent. "Not a word of enthusiasm." Delivered like a German officer. "Are you homeless, Mister Vollmer?"

"Got a place. It sucks."

"You are," Dietz hesitated, "in danger?"

"Nah." Vollmer shook his head. "I got stuff. What's in my room when I go, best still be there when I get back."

"You fear getting robbed?"

"Don't fear shit." Vollmer said it like a knife was to his throat and the knife was gonna lose. "Ain't got time to waste killing motherfuckers who rip me off."

Vollmer and Yula lay in his bed. They'd fucked twice so far tonight. Both lay on their backs, arms outspread above their heads, not touching each other and not needing to, worn out in ecstasy.

Vollmer looked at the ceiling. "You should quit that fuckin' junk."

Yula turned her head in his direction. "You should quit fuckin' stealin'. What're we, saints now?"

"I can love a whore," Vollmer said. "I can't love a junkie."

Yula sat up fast. "What the fuck?" She braced herself, both hands on the mattress. "Love? Whore? Junkie?"

Vollmer stayed on his back, looked up at her. "You're a whore, and you're a junkie. You stay like that, love won't last."

Yula turned, swung at Vollmer's face.

He caught her wrist in a fist, halfway to him. "I been hit enough. Don't." He sat up, pulled her hand farther down, close to the mattress.

She tugged hard, didn't come close to pulling her hand free, twisted halfway around then turned back fast, swung the other hand.

Vollmer caught it the same as the first, halfway to its target, held it tight. "You don't wanna hit me."

Yula struggled with both hands, her lips tight. Sad eyes didn't cry. "You said love."

Vollmer let go, and both her hands flopped by her sides. He shook his head. "Okay if you work. But that shit..." He brought his fingers down, covered a needle mark on her arm. "I ain't dyin' young. I want you forever. Get clean."

Yula's eyes went wide on his and all the color faded from them, from beautiful to gray. "You love me." She laughed but stopped short, like a cough. "You love me." A mumble. "I fuck everyone the same. You just pay better."

Vollmer's bare hand slammed across her mouth before he knew it. She fell back on the bed and bled from her lips.

"Yula!" He rolled, flung his legs around either side of hers and sat up on his knees. He leaned down to look at her face.

Yula's eyes widened and an arm swung wide and smacked Vollmer across one cheek. He didn't try to block it but turned his head, lessened the impact.

He put his thumb under her chin, fingers rested against her cheek. Yula turned away fast. He moved both hands to her shoulders, held her loose. He talked soft. "You don't love me, I gotta know."

"Ain't I don't love you. It's you callin' me shit I ain't, wantin' me to do stuff I won't."

Yeah, Vollmer thought, except it is what you are. "You think what you do, you only do to you. You keep doin' it, that's how it'll be."

"What? You think we gonna live happy ever after? And I'm fuckin' with that?"

Vollmer didn't answer, just looked down at her.

"I gotta fix my face. This best not hurt my looks."

Vollmer moved aside.

Yula swung both legs off the bed and stood. "Sometimes you act like a man, but you're still a boy. You got fuckin' dreams, and you gotta be asleep for that."

Vollmer came up the ranks fast. In an industry of square-jawed men he was angular, athletic. He still saw Yula but she didn't stay with him. Didn't matter if he had money, she had to whore those streets and she had to shoot that junk. He worked different streets now, streets where there was more money, but none of the girls on those money streets looked as good as Yula. Or fucked as good.

He still wanted Yula, but she went the way he knew she'd go. She stopped being beautiful, got to where you could find the pretty features but they were beneath everything else. Junk. Fuck junk. Dealers weren't the problem, they were guys with jobs and their bosses worked for Vollmer's boss, it was all making money. It was people, fucking weak people. Vollmer left Yula behind and he knew this weird part of him loved her, loved what she was, knew that feeling should be in the past and knew it would never leave him.

It had been a year since he walked away from her, and he was getting work out of town. Tenny jobs, and not all of Tenny's friends were local. Sometimes those friends needed help on a job, were shorthanded last minute. Vollmer was young but had a talent for improvisation, also for good judgment. As violent as required.

Tenny's idea of a friend was a man with money and needs. The most money nearby was north, in San Francisco, where sometimes a dispute was best settled by someone from out of town. These jobs were never hits, although killing was always a possibility.

"You go up there," Rico told him the first time, "they got men can do what you do. They busy or can't touch this guy, some reason. You wanna scare a guy in San Francisco? Take him to East Oakland. Way east. Don't kill him, don't shoot him. Anything besides a shooting, cops there got no time to care. Call 9-1-1 in Oakland, you get a fuckin' busy signal."

They were always muscle jobs, those out-of-towners, specialty jobs that Vollmer handled easy. Went back home to his usual, but if Rico called that took priority. Local orders still came from Williams.

Vollmer stayed street level. He didn't rank like Rico or even Williams, but guys like Williams didn't outrank him much anymore. Couldn't act like they did or he'd fuck 'em up. At that level, Rico had his back and everyone knew it.

One night he got a call to meet Williams the next morning. His meets with Williams were always in cafés, eleven a.m., at an outdoor table. A cool morning, no one else outside. Williams sat, leather jacket unzipped, back to the wall, a coffee in his hand.

Vollmer sat down across from him.

"You want coffee?" Williams asked. "Gotta order inside."

"Don't need nothin'. I'm sixteen." Vollmer grinned. No one liked Vollmer's grin.

Williams tapped the lip of his cup with the underside of thick fingers. "Get something anyway. Looks weird you don't."

Vollmer hesitated but it was Williams. Don't fuck

with the man over little shit. He went in and ordered a coffee, came back out with it and sat. "So."

Williams shook his head. "Never had a man say no to coffee."

"Ain't why I'm here."

"Got a problem. Need you to take care of it. Permanent. You in?"

"Sure," Vollmer said.

"Stone will get you the details."

This was a hit, so the order was Tenny's. Details were always delivered by men who mattered less.

He thought he could handle anything. This was different—his first hit. And it was someone he knew, he hadn't expected that. Overeager, he had to wind down. Get back to relaxed like usual. But he didn't have a usual way of getting relaxed. Just one old habit he figured would work.

He waited until dark and cruised the streets for her. It was where she'd be. Unless she'd already killed herself.

Took a while but he found what was left of her. Skinnier, less attractive, but still pretty enough to make money. She might not have long for these streets though. Uglier whores worked other parts of town.

He pulled over, rolled down a window. "Yula."

"Vollmer."

He unlocked the door and she got in.

She looked pretty good on the sidewalk, a little worse in the car. He'd take her home anyway, hope with closed eyes he could fuck a memory.

Hope wasn't something that worked for him much.

They got to his place and fucked but it wasn't like before. Not awful. She still reminded him of who she'd been.

Yula looked up at him in bed. Her eyes were fucked up but not like she'd just shot up, just like these days maybe she always looked fucked up. She lay there and parted her lips like she was going to say something.

Vollmer waited long enough. "You got somethin' to say? Or we just a whore and a john?"

"Fuck you." Yula said it casual, like a greeting.

Vollmer rolled to her, put a hand on her hip like it was what it used to be. But now it was a skinny thing.

"You won't quit the shit." He smacked at her arm with a light backhand. "And I ain't never startin' on it. A whore and a john. Except in a year you gonna be too goddamn ugly for anyone to pay."

"Fuck you." She didn't bother slapping at him.

"You ain't gotta kill yourself. That's all I'm sayin'."

Yula rolled away, turned her back on him. "Fuck you know."

"This shit gonna kill you, one way or the other." Vollmer found his cigarettes, shook one loose and lit it.

Yula turned her head over her shoulder. "Gimme one a those."

Vollmer passed her one. Yula turned her head enough for him to light it. The pose wasn't seductive. She turned away again, smoked, left a bare shoulder exposed to him.

Vollmer gripped the skinny shoulder, once so sexy. "You gonna choose how you die?"

Yula shook her shoulder and Vollmer let it go. Her head went face down in the pillow. She didn't talk. She snored. Lightly, dainty girl that she was.

He'd kick her out in the morning, get a good breakfast alone. He had a guy to kill.

Vollmer liked the guy, didn't know why he had to go. He knew a Denny's that still had a pay phone, called from there. Rolled straight to message.

"Hey Chilly. It's Vollmer. Got a extra Warriors ticket. Wanna drive up with me?"

He hung up, stayed by the phone. Chilly never picked up. Too many calls he didn't want. Vollmer felt that like a heartbeat. Why talk to fucks you don't wanna know?

The phone rang and Vollmer answered. "Yeah."

"Heard what you said." The voice was low, like he rolled out of bed. It was 2 p.m. "Got a thing tonight. Can't go."

"Game's tomorrow." Vollmer waved at the waitress bringing a slice of pie to his table. "Pick you up this time, we beat traffic."

"Yeah," Chilly said. "Sounds good."

He still sounded like he just woke up. Whatever made him sound that way, probably why he had to go.

These days Chilly did alright, rented a house with a driveway, but it was a one car drive and Chilly's Camaro was all that fit in it. Mid-afternoon in the suburbs and people weren't home from work yet. Vollmer parked just down the street. Pistol holstered on his hip, under his jacket, he walked up to the door, right hand on the pistol, and rang the bell.

Chilly took his time getting to the door. Vollmer pulled the pistol up a little, stepped out of the doorway as Chilly finally opened up.

Chilly stuck his head out. "Vollmer?"

He was drunk. Vollmer holstered his pistol and put an arm around his friend. "Chilly!"

"A minute," Chilly said, "gotta take a piss." He turned and went back into the house.

Vollmer followed, in case. Crazy men do crazy shit, and Chilly might be crazy. Some reason this job was ordered. Hell, this lazy fuck got a house somehow.

He followed Chilly to the bathroom. Chilly swung the door behind him. Vollmer stuck a hand up, stopped the door from shutting, watched Chilly piss.

Chilly turned. Vollmer was still there.

"Thought I had to go," Vollmer said. "Nah."

"Piss before we drive," Chilly said.

"I'm drivin'. I'm fine."

The drive up was 17 to the 880, but rush hour hadn't started. They made good time, got near the Coliseum.

"Shit," Vollmer said, "now I gotta take a piss."

Chilly looked at the clock on the car stereo. "Pull over anywhere. We got plenty a time."

Vollmer nodded, like thanks for permission, got off the freeway a couple off-ramps later. He made his way down a near empty street, pulled over, and walked around the back of the car.

He came up to the passenger door, opened it, held his Browning on Chilly. "Get out."

"Vollmer?" Chilly's eyes widened and his hands went to the driver's seat, like there was some way to escape.

Vollmer opened the door and leaned in, grabbed Chilly by the shirt collar, yanked, not much luck so he put a hand behind Chilly's neck, turned a hip and threw him out of the car.

25

Chilly scraped his hands bloody on the street, didn't make a sound about that, looked up and saw the barrel of Vollmer's pistol two feet from his forehead. "Aaahhh!"

Too much noise, Chilly, shut up, shut up.

Chilly kept screaming.

Vollmer unloaded, one to the head, two to the head, everything he had to the head.

Chilly shut up.

Vollmer turned the car around, headed back home. He needed something now, something he couldn't have. He'd go home for whatever it was, nothing could put him in Oakland tonight. This was fucked up. He liked Chilly. And Rico could have got anyone to take him out. He chose Vollmer because Vollmer knew Chilly. Not because that made it easy to set up the hit. It was a test to see if he'd kill a friend, to see if he'd do whatever they wanted. He passed, so long as he got away clean. That's what he was doing now.

He rolled down the front windows, needed air. Part of him felt good, killing was a rush, he wanted to burst or stop breathing altogether. The freeway would be better. Home would be better.

He reached the 880 and let the engine out a little, but he couldn't go as fast as he wanted, couldn't get a ticket, couldn't put himself anywhere but home tonight. Evidence of Chilly in his car meant nothing, Chilly had been in his car before. So long as nothing put him near the murder. He drove toward home but what did home mean? A safe place to sleep? He couldn't sleep tonight, he needed more than that. And he wasn't a drugs and booze guy. A drink might be alright, even two to level him out, but he couldn't wind down much that way. Hell, he wanted to celebrate.

Vollmer got off 17, checked the gas. Plenty for local driving. He hit those old streets, the ones where the whores ran. It was early but it was dark, they were out. Three streets she might be on, the same few blocks of each. Drove down one, then up the next. He knew what she was like now. Still the best he could do.

Vollmer cruised all three blocks, twice, three times, pulled over when he saw a spot. Fuck. He just wanted to ball her brains out. Her or someone better, but he didn't know no one better.

He looked up and down the street. Where were all the goddamn whores? Not on this block. After a couple minutes, he got out and walked. One good thing about being on the sidewalk, he could get a better look at the girls. A lot of them looked good from a passing car, didn't look so good up close. He'd driven past a few of those already. He knew those girls and he'd fucked a few of them, but this was a special night. He wanted his special whore.

There was no number to call, it was always a find her situation. Nights he couldn't find her she was doing too well to want to be found. It was a weeknight. He had a chance. Also a chance she'd disappoint. She wasn't what she used to be. Not the person, not even the whore. Still pretty though.

He saw legs up the block, a skirt too short to be anything but an invitation. He walked straight ahead, got closer. There was a shape to the legs that Yula's no longer had. A different girl, a blonde, or at least a blonde wig. He got close and she turned her head. She saw him, stepped back. Johns were never on the sidewalk. The blonde was pretty, a white girl, and her cheeks weren't caved in. A little round still. Vollmer was okay with white girls. He'd fucked them before.

"Hey," he said. He wasn't dressed great, probably looked as tired as a man who'd just killed a friend.

The blonde didn't talk, darted her eyes to the street, where a car with a real john might come from.

"I got a car and a place," Vollmer said. "And I pay better than whoever shows up next. You don't wanna walk with me to the car, I get it. I wouldn't walk with me. I'm goin' to the car. Wait here."

She stood there, still wordless, looked at him at least as long as he looked at her.

Vollmer turned away, walked back to his car. End of the block he looked back. The blonde watched the street for cars. The safe play. He walked faster.

Vollmer turned his car around, drove back to the blonde. Gone. It wasn't that she was too pretty for him. He gave her a choice, the sure thing or the long shot, and the sure thing showed up first. His mistake. He was hazy after shooting Chilly, never should've gave the whore a choice. If he wanted her he should've taken her. Maybe he didn't really want her. If he didn't, it was because he preferred a Yula who no longer existed. He should have grabbed the blonde, took her to his place, paid her and fucked her. Instead he made himself a guy on the sidewalk who says he has money.

He drove the blocks again. The blonde woulda been nice. He's gonna explode. If it ain't a whore, he don't know what.

He might run out of gas driving these same blocks over and over, but he didn't wanna miss out on another girl like that. Plenty of other girls out there, but he was back to the consolation prizes he wouldn't settle for. After an hour, he pulled over. The passenger side window was already down. "Get in."

A skinny black girl leaned through the open window. "Hey baby."

Vollmer looked at her. "Get in. This ain't fast or cheap." He laughed like that would make everything lower key, but the whore recoiled. "Rough day," he said. "I need some time. You get paid."

She sat next to him with a big smile. "I'm Alicia."

Chilly was his first hit but wasn't the first man he killed, wouldn't be the last. But Vollmer never killed a friend before. He didn't smile back at the whore, just pulled his car into the street and headed to his place.

They got there without a word. "I don't talk much," he said, and unlocked the car doors. "Nothin' against you." He looked her up and down. "I like you."

She smiled again. "We don't gotta talk. Unless you want."

He walked her inside. Her skin looked soft, but he didn't touch it yet. She was a stranger. He wanted everything new when they fucked.

He led her to the bed.

"Pay before play," she said.

He unsnapped the top button of his jeans, reached into a pocket and pulled out a fistful of bills, peeled off five twenties and handed them to her.

"Do this good enough," he said, "there's more when we're done. But don't even think about ripping me off. I earned that shit."

"We good." She walked to the bed and stopped. "You want me naked any way special?"

"Take it off."

The clothes came off just slow enough, a beautiful display. Her small breasts were pert, shapely, a lean but strong-looking abdomen beneath, her bare skin a rich brown color, something that had to be touched with both hands and tongue. He'd seen most of the legs already, didn't need to look at her feet or pussy.

She looked damn good naked, just a little thin.

"On the bed," he said. "On your belly."

She lay down, her head turned back as he squatted over her. His knees straddled her ass cheeks. He leaned to his left, opened the bedside table drawer, grabbed an already cut length of rope and quickly tied her hands behind her back.

"Hey!"

Vollmer didn't answer, just pushed down hard on her upper back with one hand, immobilizing her as the other hand ran up and down her thighs, squeezing the fleshiest pieces, then moved up to her ass and did the same.

"Let me up!"

He stopped pressing down and rubbed both palms along her back, then reached around to feel her tits and belly with one hand, covered her mouth with the other. His pants were off and a rubber on as he clung to one breast and fucked her. She didn't have to be scared but he knew why she was and he wasn't stopping. He fucked her and fucked her and fucked her and too bad she was scared. He didn't make her that way. The rope stayed on but she was a whore and that's what he was paying for. He didn't need the rope with Yula, he did with everyone else. He thought he'd come any second, right from when they started, but it went on and he let go of her back, turned her head so he could look at her face as he slammed into her ass over and over. This was all he wanted and everything he was getting away from, no more killing friends only fucking strangers. He came suddenly and let go of her head as he collapsed onto her back, exhausted but only a minute.

He rolled off her, onto his back, reached into the bedside table's open drawer, pulled out a knife.

The whore screamed.

"No one can hear you." He rolled toward her with the knife and cut the rope, loosened it so her hands fell free. He closed the knife, rolled back to the drawer and dropped it and the rope back inside, withdrew a thick stack of bills.

"Sit up."

It took a minute but she caught her breath and sat.

Vollmer held out five twenties like it was a royal flush. Then did the same with the other hand. "That's for the fucking."

She grabbed the two hundred dollars fast as she could and moved to the far end of the bed.

"Wait."

She already stood, on her way to the next customer, walked around the bed, got her clothes on fast, and walked toward the door.

Vollmer held out two more twenties. "You want cab fare, don'tcha?"

She snatched them like they'd bite and stormed out.

He lay in bed in the dark room, stared up at a ceiling he couldn't see. Knowing Rico and Williams played him. Man, they played him. Chilly, that dumb kid. Vollmer blinked fast a few times, stared up at the black ceiling again. But it wasn't like he could have said no to the job. A man could turn down a hit, but not once he got the details.

Stone had told him the name at Williams's usual coffee table.

"Ah fuck." Vollmer shook his head.

"First time I seen you react," Stone said. "To anything. You know him?"

Vollmer didn't say shit.

"They know you do. Part of why. Man need to go away, you can't be makin' choices."

Vollmer stood. "If he gotta die, he gotta die."

He drove, looked for Yula or any whore good enough to replace her for a night. He'd already fucked but he was seventeen, and after killing Chilly he needed more. He needed a thing that wasn't there—a rush greater than what you feel after you kill a friend.

Nothing was gonna wipe that away. Vollmer drove ready to kill again. He was never ready to kill Chilly, he just put himself where he had to. Vollmer thought back to when he'd pulled the pistol, the look in Chilly's eyes. A look of betrayal, like a man would never kill a friend. Like Chilly didn't get the whole thing. Cross Tenny and you die, it don't matter what anyone else wants. Vollmer didn't betray anyone. He kept himself alive.

Vollmer was pissed anyway. Chilly was dead, and the next man who got in his way was deader. Slower, harder, he wouldn't know until he was doing it. Right now he needed to fuck again, blow off steam. Explode inside someone instead of on them. He needed to fuck and he needed to kill. He'd done both too recently for either need to be urgent. They were.

Vollmer drove past the whores. Some of them looked

pretty good, but not good enough. He'd had another girl and she just made him want Yula again. No one else measured up. Yula wasn't what she'd been but she was a part of him. If there was any of her left, he was part of her too.

Up a street, down a street, a couple hours and there she was. Where she'd been the last couple hours he didn't care; she was his now. He pulled over, rolled down the passenger side window.

"Yula. Get in."

She looked at him and smiled. "Hey baby." She opened the door and sat down.

The smile looked like maybe she didn't remember who he was. The door shut and Vollmer pulled away from the curb.

Not like a house and kids, he wouldn't do that, but they coulda been good together. For a while at least. They used to talk. A little, anyway. Enough.

Enough to know there was something besides junk in her veins.

Only a couple days since the last time he saw her. She must not have been high then.

Now they rode. Her hand too busy scratching her own flesh to bother with provoking his. If she was the Yula he knew before, Vollmer would have pulled over and they'd have dealt with this by now. And there'd be more later. Instead it was like a zombie beside him, mumbling to herself while he tried to ignore it. The girl he'd wanted had become this woman. He'd known she would. He hadn't known how soon.

"Yula." She'd finally thought of putting her hand on his thigh, did it in a halting, drunken manner. He picked up the hand and dropped it on her own leg. "This is nothin' but a fuck. Let's get it good as we can. You get paid."

"Don't be like that, baby. I know you, Vollmer. I know you good."

There was no conversation this could turn into. "We go to my place."

"You look good, baby. Things goin' good?"

Everything was good with her. At least the way she talked. Not the way she lived. "We go to my place," he said. "And fuck. That's all."

Yula shook her head, smiled in a way that used to be sexy, stroked his inner thigh up to his dick. That still worked. He drove to his place, eager to get this over with.

She was still pretty good with her clothes off, not as smooth or round as before but a body better than most. The way she moved was the way she was, fucked up, but he could close his eyes and suck her tits and almost think she was the same girl. He fucked her hard as he could and damn near burst that condom, opened his eyes and her face was so pretty. Then she opened her eyes and he saw no one.

He rolled off, thought of Chilly. That was what this was supposed to get rid of. "Jesus."

"Good, huh?"

Vollmer closed his eyes and wished she wasn't there. He'd rather be alone with the shit in his head. It was fucking Chilly's fault. Someone was gonna pull the trigger, it just happened to be him. Had to be him, because that's what Rico wanted.

"Yeah," he said, like Yula heard him right and she

was still God's gift to whores, but that wasn't close to what this was about.

"There's nothing to drink here," Vollmer said, and got out of bed. He picked up his pants from the floor and put them on. "Tonight I could use one."

"We could get somethin'." Yula sat up in bed. "Come back here after."

She'd already been paid once, now she was working on twice. At least she was still good at her job.

His head was a mess, a drink sounded good. He knew that was wrong. That's what old fuckups did, tried to clear their heads with shit that muddied it. But a little might take the edge off. That's all he wanted, not enough to get fucked up.

"Maybe." Vollmer put on his T-shirt. "Let's get outta here, at least get some air." No way in hell he was coming back here with her. Maybe sometime, but not tonight. He drove with Yula beside him and he knew too well what fucked up was.

Vollmer dropped off Yula at a corner she liked to work, lied and said he no longer wanted a drink. Mainly he didn't want to drink with her.

He drove a lot of blocks from where he dropped her. He knew guys who'd give him a bottle if he asked; no idea where they'd be this time of night. Easiest to do this the old fashioned way. Hang out near a liquor store, ask a stranger. But he hated asking for help.

Vollmer stood at the back of a parking lot. It was a mini mall, most of the stores closed by now. The pizza place took up a lot of the parking, the liquor store got the rest. After a few minutes a guy parked and stepped toward the liquor store.

Vollmer walked fast, greeted the stranger. "Hey,

buddy." He held out his hand, a twenty in it. "Buy me a pint a Jack?"

The stranger looked at him hard. "Lose your ID?"

"You a cop?"

The stranger took a step back. "Just wonderin'."

Vollmer reached into his pocket, pulled out another twenty. "Get yourself somethin' too."

The stranger relaxed a little, took both twenties, walked into the liquor store.

Vollmer stood in the middle of the lot and waited. The stranger came out with a plastic bag that held a six pack and then some. He got to Vollmer and handed him the pint of Jack.

Vollmer wanted a slug right then but he took it to the car, set it on the seat beside him, where Yula's ass had been. He drove it back to his place, wanted a shot every second of the drive. Not with her. He killed the man alone, he'd drink to him alone.

Got home, opened the bottle, no glass, got the cap open and drank. Chilly. Fucking Chilly.

"That kid Vollmer." Williams sat at his usual outdoor café table. He was huge, even compared to Rico, who sat across from him. It was clear that didn't matter, Rico ran this show. "He got heart."

Rico looked up from his coffee. "Or no heart. In a good way." He'd waited a week before arranging the meeting, wanted to make sure about Vollmer. He laughed, and Williams laughed with him. Nothing in the world was funny.

"He's a kid," Williams said, "but he's maybe the coldest man I know."

"Since that thing with his friend, right?"

"Yeah," Williams said.

"Thought that'd work. Kid had potential."

"The kid's great on the job," Williams said, "but I can't trust him."

Rico waved a hand, a slow motion karate chop over his coffee. "You ain't got to, he don't work for you no more. The kid's mine."

Williams's eyes widened, but he wasn't dumb enough to question Rico. Vollmer was either promoted or out completely, that was Rico's call. Williams sipped his coffee, but this kind of relief called for a shot.

Williams nodded. "He'd never say no, even before. Now? Worse it is, more he wants it."

Rico drank coffee, set his cup down. "Most men, think they don't give a fuck, you can find a point they do. Get 'em past that early?" Rico smiled. "He scare you?"

Williams shook his head. "Glad he's on our side, though."

"Came to us a soldier. We make him stronger. You got how many boys? Three?"

"Yeah. But none in the life."

"I got none I know," Rico said. "Don't know where they are, gotta be some is all. But these? Kids like Vollmer? They're my children. And our children are our future." Rico laughed alone at that, laughed hard.

Rico met Vollmer in a restaurant. Rico chose El Charrito—good Mexican food and a full bar. He had a Negra Modelo and an empty shot glass in front of him when the kid walked in.

Vollmer sat down.

Rico raised a hand, snapped fingers, loud. "You want anything?"

"I work for you?"

"What I'm findin' out."

"It's what I want," Vollmer said.

The place was packed but a waitress got there quick.

"One more of these." Rico waved his hand over his beer bottle and shot glass. "And whatever he wants."

She looked at Vollmer.

"Coke," he said. "And some chips. Salsa."

Rico grinned. "Bring a menu, hon."

The waitress nodded and smiled. She was pretty, busty, showed it off. "Yes, sir."

She walked away.

Rico watched, turned his eyes back to Vollmer. "Rellenos if you're hungry. Great fuckin' rellenos. Just want an appetizer? You could have Renata," he nodded toward the waitress, "for your main course."

Vollmer's mouth was stern. "I fuck after I work."

"Fine, but you ain't findin' girls on the job. You pissed at me, Vollmer?"

"Ain't pissed at no one."

Rico finished his beer. "Don't look happy."

"Lookin' for work is all. Don't think Williams is gonna use me no more. Don't want him to. Glad you called."

"Glad." Rico shook his head.

Renata came back with a tray, set down the drinks for Rico and Vollmer, then the chips and salsa, handed Vollmer a menu and walked away.

Rico watched again, raised his tequila and downed the shot. He smiled, more hungry than happy. "You show glad funny."

"Did what Williams wanted, now he thinks I'm crazy. I work for you or I work alone." His lips turned up a little at last. "You got some crazy work for me?"

"You want crazy?" Rico drank beer. "You work for me now. You get paid every week. Some weeks might not be much work. Some weeks a lot. One thing on crazy shit. I gotta okay it. I can change it from crazy to smart."

Rico drank.

Vollmer washed down some chips with his Coke, gave a real smile. "So you got somethin' crazy already?"

Rico shook his head. "Dangerous is all. Not crazy. Smart."

Other men didn't want the work Vollmer got, and Vollmer didn't want the work other men got. Funny that Rico called it dangerous. Wasn't dangerous for Vollmer. Dangerous for anyone who got in his way.

Months of this work. Could turn to years easy. He liked the job.

He didn't smile much, even after post-job fucks. Losing Yula was one thing—he'd seen that coming. But since he killed Chilly everything felt like revenge, and whoever he saw was to blame. He knew it most when he looked in the mirror.

He supposed it was good he didn't drink much. The world was dark enough. He couldn't dwell on it, and he couldn't improve it. He could miss the one friend he'd had. Chilly. And he missed Yula.

He looked for her at night sometimes, knew he shouldn't, the way she lived. If he saw her on the street and nothing had changed, he'd turn away. She might be dead by now. She might be worse. He looked for her anyway.

"A lotta tough guys," Rico said to Williams, "they got a crazy gear. That's how they handle tough guys who ain't crazy. What I like about Vollmer, ain't no gears to shift."

"Nah," Williams said, "he's always crazy." Williams downed his shot and tapped the bar for another. From his huge hand even a tap resounded. The bartender looked his way.

"That ain't it," Rico said. "He's always there." He twirled a finger outside an ear. "And however he gets in, he's walkin' out, so he can walk back in again."

"How's that scare a crazy man?"

The bartender was there already, poured fresh shots for both men.

Rico drank beer while the bartender poured, waited until he walked away. "Didn't you come up a crazy man? Biggest, baddest dude in town?"

Williams nodded. "Smart too, though."

Rico smiled. "Too smart to want Vollmer working for you."

"That's sense. That ain't fear."

"You always had sense," Rico said. "You still got crazy, right?"

"Much as I need."

"Need," Rico said. "A weakness Vollmer ain't got. He just is. And no one wants to find out everything he is."

* * *

Stone was the guy he ran with now when he found a two-man job. Not that Stone exactly ran, had a hitch in his walk from an old football injury. Not an organized game, a game of tackle in the street that broke three bones in his foot, aggravated when he stepped on it wrong running from a guy he tried to mug.

Damn good with a heavy pistol, at the shooting range he let Vollmer practice with his Glock .50.

"You gonna love this weapon," Stone said. "Show it and most of the time you won already. Looks like a fucking cannon. And if you gotta use it? You kill some-one, you take out the wall behind them."

"Fuck." Vollmer felt the power when he fired that pistol, loved shooting the thing. Had to have one.

"Hook me up with one of these," he said to Stone, "what's it gonna cost?"

"Not much," Stone said, "if you got a job we pull together after you get yours."

"Get a box of cartridges with it. I'm always lookin' for work."

Only a week and Stone called him up. Vollmer never hosted a meeting; they met at Williams's outdoor café.

Stone sat across from Vollmer. "You order inside?"

Vollmer shook his head. "No waitresses here, I just sat down."

Stone nodded. "They sell drinks?"

"Coffee, tea, I don't know what else."

"Fuck that. You find a job?"

"Yeah," Vollmer said. No one was at the tables around them. Vollmer kept his voice low anyway. "Two man. High risk, high reward. You get what I ordered?"

"In my car. We should go for a ride."

"Okay," Vollmer said. "But I only talk outdoors."

Stone's eyes widened, like it wasn't an answer he'd expect from a teenager.

Vollmer got that look a lot, like he knew shit a guy his age shouldn't. Probably a good thing. He figured people shouldn't know what he knew as a kid. Bad enough he knew. He made that bad work for him.

They drove out of the city, past everything. It wasn't a big city but they kept going and where they got to had to be nowhere—no people, no buildings, just a two-lane road with trees and hills on either side.

No reason for a hit, Vollmer hadn't done anything to deserve that, but he could reach his pistol fast if he had to. More likely Stone was mic'd, but Vollmer already told him he wouldn't talk in the car. And he'd never say who ordered a job. Shit, Stone knew that. What the fuck was up with this? His right hand rested, fingers bent on his thigh, ready to grab the Browning 9 from inside his coat.

Stone pulled off the main road and down a narrow path into the woods. Odds of someone dying went up. No one would hear a fucking bomb out here. Stone stopped the car at a spot out of view from the main road, got out of the car.

He walked to the trunk, lifted its lid. "Come on."

Fuck it, he liked Stone. Vollmer got out of the car, hand inside his jacket, took a wide turn around the back of the car.

Stone held a Glock .50 by the barrel, handed it to Vollmer.

Vollmer's empty hand came out of his jacket, then he was turning the pistol over in both hands. "Man." It was gorgeous, new. It shined.

"Think fast."

Vollmer looked up, felt like a fucking idiot for letting his guard down, but it was a holster in mid-air. He caught it with one hand, held the Glock with the other.

"Got 'em to throw it in," Stone said. "Didn't know if you had one that'd hold this."

"Cartridges?" Vollmer asked, alert again.

"One box in the trunk. Go through it on the range, buy more. Takes a while to aim this thing straight."

Vollmer nodded. They were gonna take some money with a pair of these. Maybe kill some motherfuckers too. "Let's go now. The range."

Stone and Vollmer in black leather jackets, dark pants, similar builds and each with a Glock .50, could have been twins to the people they ripped off. The kind of guys who'd look dangerous without weapons. A year plus of doing jobs together and they even moved alike, except for Stone's limp.

Stone was older but Vollmer ran every show. A criminal since childhood, it was all natural to him: where to look for hidden money, which victim needed a pistol whipping to know they meant business, that sort of thing.

Then came a chance at real money. Some dumb fuck name of Delmas skimmed money from Tenny and Tenny didn't know yet.

"You sure?" Stone asked. "How much?"

Vollmer nodded. "Guy who told me wouldn't lie. Not to me. How much?" Vollmer shrugged. "Don't matter. We get it back to Tenny before he knows it's gone. Then we're noticed. That matters."

Vollmer had been watching Delmas a while. His plan

was simple. Delmas took a briefcase to his bank every Thursday, always went to a safe deposit box. They'd shake him down on the sidewalk one Thursday afternoon when he left his office, which was on a block barren as a ghost town. They wouldn't get a lot of his money that way, but enough for Rico to convince Tenny. Tenny'd get the rest somehow.

Vollmer waited just outside Delmas's building, Stone down the street near Delmas's car. No one else on the sidewalk, no one driving by. Most of the cars parked down here looked as abandoned as the buildings.

Delmas came out, walked toward his car a half block away, a hulking guy beside him. They always drove to the bank together.

Vollmer gave them a few feet head start. He followed as Stone came toward them. Almost mirror images in their jackets and pants, all black, including the Glocks about to come out.

Vollmer came up tight. "Drop the case." He jammed the pistol into the back of Delmas's neck.

Delmas's head jutted forward. The case dropped. He didn't turn and neither did the hood beside him.

Ten feet in front of them, Stone pulled his Glock from under his coat, held it close but made sure they saw it.

"On the ground," Vollmer said. "Both of you."

The hood turned his head slightly and Vollmer backhanded him across the cheek with his pistol. The big man fell back, tried to catch his balance but Vollmer kicked him hard in the shin and he fell.

"Eyes to the ground," Vollmer said.

Stone stood just in front of them now, his Glock aimed at one man then the other. They lay face down.

Vollmer dropped down fast, slammed the thug's head into the sidewalk, brought a knee down hard on Delmas's back. "This is Tenny's money. Get the rest out of the bank for him or you're fucked."

He stood with the briefcase, kicked Delmas in the ribs while Stone kicked the hood in his bleeding head.

Street still empty, they walked briskly past Delmas's building to where Vollmer parked and drove back to the bodies. Vollmer popped the trunk and both men got out of the car, left their doors open. Delmas had pushed himself up on his hands and that was all. The thug lay unconscious.

Just the four of them on the sidewalk.

Stone raised the trunk the rest of the way, walked back to join Vollmer and the men on the ground. Vollmer pulled his Glock .50 from his coat and Stone did the same. They fired almost simultaneously, both shooting the hood in the head, holstered their pistols, dragged Delmas to the trunk and threw him in. Stone shut it as Delmas whimpered, and he and Vollmer got back into the car.

They slammed their doors and Vollmer floored it. Blocks away, he slowed down. "Drop you at your place?"

Stone shrugged. "Sure." They'd gone over this. Stone wanted to meet Rico but it wouldn't happen in the middle of a job. When it was over, Vollmer would get word to Rico who his partner was. And Stone would move up the chain.

Vollmer called Rico. "Got a present for your boss. Tonight."

"Now?"

45

"Yeah."

"El Charrito."

"You get there first, don't order a meal. We're leaving fast."

Rico always got there first. If he wasn't close he'd have named another place. He didn't want anyone walking in on him.

He'd downed a shot of tequila, was drinking Negra Modelo from the bottle when Vollmer joined him. "What's new?"

Vollmer sat. "You know Delmas?"

"What about him?"

"You know he was skimming?"

"Was?"

"I took today's take from him. And I took him."

"You delivering now?"

Vollmer nodded.

"Honey!" Rico yelled across the room. "Check!"

He paid cash, finished his beer, and they got out.

Drove in separate cars, Vollmer in front, meeting place decided in the parking lot. Middle of nowhere. In the hills outside of town.

Vollmer pulled over in the depths of some ugly wood, got out with a briefcase in one hand.

Rico held a .45 at his side. "That the money?"

"Gotta be. He was taking it to the bank. Ain't looked inside. But I know what bank. Delmas knows what deposit box."

"Where's he?"

Vollmer raised his chin. "The trunk."

Rico waved him over with his gun hand. Vollmer walked back there, opened it with his key. He knew better than to pop a trunk in front of Rico. Sudden sound like that, good way to get shot.

Delmas lay there, unconscious but breathing. "No blood?" Rico asked.

"Nah. Broken ribs, maybe."

"Put him in my trunk." Rico got out his keys, popped the lock.

Vollmer carried Delmas. Rico walked behind him, pistol in hand, flicked the trunk all the way open with his fingers. Vollmer dropped Delmas inside and Rico shut the trunk.

"Make my car disappear?" Vollmer asked. "Someone mighta seen it."

The car wasn't registered in Vollmer's name but he drove away from a murder and kidnap scene in it.

"Sure," Rico said. "Want a ride?"

"Hey baby, remember me?"

The voice cracked. Her face was still pretty but it had been two years and she was leaner—two years of junk faded beauty. Her legs looked stripped of meat, their once perfect shape gone, her hips with them. Her young breasts hung where two years before they'd stood. And now the taut belly was just part of a skinny junkie with nice features, not a marvel between round tits and thick thighs.

"Yula." He mumbled her name, didn't want to say more.

"I missed you, baby. We had good times together."

He looked close, saw no sign of who she used to be. "I gotta go." The street was dark. He took a step into it.

"No," she said. "Vollmer. I need your help. I'm in trouble."

He turned. It was dark on the sidewalk. There was a crowd nearby.

"Whattaya mean? Pregnant?"

Yula nodded fast, like it was a good thing. "Just need a little. I take care of it and I can work. I know you got it. I pay you back."

"Like fuck you will."

"Vollmer." She laughed, like they were a couple and he'd joke about this.

Vollmer walked away.

Yula ran at his turned back.

He spun, got his hands under her arms, lifted her. "Get the fuck away from me."

Yula whispered down at him. "I saw what you did to Delmas. Least I say I did."

She lied about that. If anyone saw he would've heard by now, but Vollmer didn't need the attention. Still, how'd anyone know besides him, Stone, and Rico? Delmas fucking disappeared.

He put her down.

"We go back to my place," he said. "We fuck like before, and I pay extra. You get what you need. I get something out of it too. And you don't bother me again."

Yula nodded and they walked away together. Up the street, to his car.

"This yours?" she asked.

"Yeah."

"It's nice."

Vollmer started the engine. "It's a fuckin' Honda. A car no one notices."

"Oh." Yula laughed.

It wasn't a joke, not close. Vollmer liked not liking her right now. "When you say you saw somethin'…What you gonna say?"

Yula tilted her head to the right, raised her eyebrows, looked like a goddamn cartoon. "Ain't sayin' nothin'. We got a agreement."

"Someone gonna put me at a crime scene, I gotta know what they sayin'."

"I ain't sayin' nothin'." She said it slow but looked scared.

"You know some hood's dead? You sayin' I got somethin' to do with that? Where'd you get that bullshit?"

"I got a story puts you with him. Don't know nothin' 'bout death."

If she didn't know the hood was dead, what bullshit was she blackmailing him with? Anyway, she knew now.

"Good to hear." Vollmer pulled into the apartment house garage. He parked, walked around to help Yula out, like it was romantic and not that she couldn't get out of the car on her own. No one saw him hustle her inside. Even if they happened to see him with a girl they couldn't say who.

He let her into his place, pushed her against the front door as he shut, locked, and bolted it. Hard from seeing hot chicks all day without fucking them, he leaned down and nibbled at her neck.

"Oh, baby." Yula ran an index finger down the front of Vollmer's shirt to his pants, down the length of his dick until she reached its head a few inches down his thigh. She dropped her hand so it hung beside her own scrawny thigh. "But we gotta do the money first."

Vollmer walked backward away from her. "Come on." He turned and she followed him through the small living room, put an arm under his coat and around him as they turned a corner down a hallway.

"Man. This is nice."

Vollmer put an arm around her too. "How much money we talkin'?"

There was a door at the end of the hall. "A couple grand should do it."

"Yeah." He let go of her, opened the door and entered the bedroom. "That'd do it."

He walked to a bedside table with a lamp on it and a drawer. "Money's in here." He looked back at Yula. "Come on."

She stood just inside the door, didn't move.

Like she didn't believe him.

His hand came out of the drawer fast, threw a handful of bills across the bed. "That should be enough. We can count it together."

As though drawn by the money, Yula walked to the bed.

Vollmer stepped behind her and threw her on it, face down.

"Count the money first," she said, but Vollmer sat on her ass and pinned her there. She turned her head as he pulled the short rope from inside the drawer.

"What," she started. Vollmer slapped her. Yula's face fell against the bed.

He got the rope around her neck and yanked it taut. She strained to get away, to breathe. He pulled the rope tighter. She struggled for breath. Struggled a minute. Then her struggles were over.

ACT 2

Tenny glared. Not that he ever looked happy, but this was worse. "He's your responsibility, Rico."

Rico's hefty palms pressed against the tabletop. The thugs on either side of Tenny each aimed a .45 at Rico's chest.

"He's mine," Rico said, his low voice at its most guttural. He'd brought Dust in, he'd take him out. He hated friends who betrayed him.

One thing Rico always knew about his collectors was where they lived while they worked for him. He knew a lot more than that about Dust. He'd actually liked the guy. Now he had to find him.

Rico left Tenny late afternoon. He sent Vollmer to watch Theresa's place. Dust had lived with Theresa most of the months he'd worked for Rico, collecting from welchers who owed Tenny. He moved out of her place a little while before he ripped off Tenny, but he'd spent all that time with the woman. Even if he didn't go back to her, she might know something.

Rico knew Olive, Dust's most recent woman, the one right after Theresa. He'd start with her. But he only

51

knew her from the bar, and they were going to hit a point where it didn't matter that he tipped good. At least it was a short drive. Dust wouldn't be dumb enough to be there, but she might know something.

He found parking not far from the building and walked to the front door, pressed every bell but Olive's. Someone would buzz him in, then he'd take the elevator to her floor. In case anyone saw him coming or going, he'd have to treat her gentler than he'd like. Rico was barrel chested, a little barrel gutted, with a flat nose and narrow eyes. People always remembered him when they saw him. He'd had to talk to a few of them about that.

A buzzer sounded. A voice said "Yeah?" Rico was already in the door.

He reached Olive's floor, then her door. Nobody answered. Rico tried the doorknob and it turned. He pushed the door open. A half inch and it hit the chain.

"Stop." It was Olive's voice. "Or I'll fucking kill you." She sounded scared.

"Olive. It's Rico. What's wrong?"

"Rico?" Now she sounded confused. "What the fuck you doin' here?"

"Lookin' for Dust. What'sa matter, honey?"

"You can't see me." Her voice fell to a near whisper. "No one can see me."

"You okay? Is it Dust?"

"Fuck Dust."

"I know," Rico said. "He's in trouble. He hurt you?"

"Trouble?"

"You wanna let me in?" Rico said. "We can talk, maybe have a drink."

"You can't come in."

"You wanna get a drink somewhere? We gotta talk, I

gotta find Dust. Our boy's in trouble."

"I can't go out."

"Then lemme in. I won't hurtcha."

"That's what I thought about Dust." Olive shut the door, took a second and opened it with the chain down, enough for Rico to see her.

Olive's face was red and swollen along one cheek, up to her eye and back to her ear. There were thin marks at the point of impact but they weren't bleeding, just evidence. No way Olive called the cops or she'd be at the station or the hospital. And if she hadn't called then, she'd never call. Next chance she gave a man, he'd kill her or she'd kill him.

And she knew Rico and Dust were friends, had to assume Rico was a criminal too, but she was desperate enough to see him. He could only figure it was fear. Whatever the reason, he was glad for it. He liked Olive, she was a nice bartender and a hot, thin, Italian chick, but what really mattered now was he needed her. She had to know something about Dust.

"He hit you?" Rico said. He stayed in the hall, waited for Olive to step back, invite him in.

"With a glass. A nice drinking glass."

Drunk fuck. "He always did..."

"I told him he drank too much. That's what pissed him off. I dunno, he was already pissed off."

"Dust gets outta hand, ain't the first time. Invite me in, Olive, have a drink. That boy needs help."

Olive nodded, stepped back, let Rico in. He shut the door behind him, got a good look at her as she turned away and walked to the tiny kitchen. Her face was still half beautiful.

Just beyond the kitchen lay a room almost as small.

A couch with a computer next to it and a TV nearby, not much room for anything else. Down something that barely counted as a hall he saw two more doors.

Olive came back with two glasses. "Bourbon alright?"

Rico nodded.

Olive lifted her chin to the small couch. Rico took a seat on one end.

Olive walked around, handed Rico his glass and sat down at the opposite end, one cushion between them.

Rico chose the side where if Olive didn't face him she'd show her damaged profile. She turned to look at him and they drank.

"Dust," Rico said, "was already pissed off when you argued?"

"He bitched a lot about how stressful his job was. He never told me how, said I couldn't know."

Dust wasn't a guy who'd talk about his work, knew better, but that's what men do with women they stay with. And a man who drinks like Dust...if he hadn't pulled this bullshit with Tenny, Rico never would've thought it. But the man might've talked. "He said somethin' 'bout the job stressed him?"

"He never said what. He bitched, but he never explained. There was no way to have a conversation."

"And you pushed him on that and he hit you?"

"No! He got too drunk and he was an asshole. I told him that, told him to get his shit fixed or get out and he fucking went off. On me." She let the words tail off like she was about to cry, took a drink instead.

Rico drank too. He let Olive bring her glass down before he lowered his. Like they were friends drinking together. "I know Dust a lotta years. He goes off the deep end like this, I can bring him back. But I gotta know where he is."

Olive's eyes were on her drink. "I told him get out. I didn't say where."

"And he left?" Rico raised his eyebrows.

"He hurt me. He left."

Still bourbon in her glass. Olive looked at it, Rico looked at her. She drank.

"You think," Rico said, "he felt guilty."

Olive nodded, her glass empty now, and stood. "Another?"

Rico downed what remained in his glass and she took it from him.

Olive came back with full glasses, handed Rico his and sipped as she sat. "He never talked bad about the woman he was with before. That was nice, if it meant he'd treat me the same. Coulda meant he still liked her, though. And there's Val down south, he talked about how he used to protect her. Like he didn't anymore. Like he was sad about it."

"He talk about anyone else?"

Olive shook her head. "Dust didn't talk. He liked to drink and fuck. The two don't go together so good."

"Yeah," Rico said. "With some people, they don't."

It was the sort of line Olive might think was a pickup. It wasn't, but Rico didn't mind putting it out there. Not now, but sometime if she was up for it. Sometime wouldn't come if he didn't find Dust.

Olive spoke over the lip of her glass. "Drinkers don't need to like who they drink with."

Rico shook his head. He didn't want Olive defensive. "Dust liked you. He fucks things up."

He'd already asked for her help. He wouldn't ask

again, not yet. She had to know he was on her side. It was possible she didn't know more about Dust than she'd already said. Dust did stupid shit, but he never talked about anything important. No matter who he was with he always acted like he might wind up in prison again, with no one to protect him, and with one wrong word you wrote your own death warrant. He made alliances when he was inside—Rico had been one of his allies, that's where they met—but after he got out Dust did his time alone.

"Call me, wouldja?" Rico got a card from his wallet. "Leave a message if you think of something. Ain't my number, but I'll hear what you say."

"Yeah." She sounded sad, sexy as hell, lost in a dream of what she'd thought she and Dust could be.

Rico drank slow, gave Olive a chance to continue. She didn't. He got up with his drink. "I gotta tear the place apart now. Help with that, it's easier to put back together."

Olive got up, a look on her face like she'd never seen Rico before, like he and Dust just showed her the world.

Rico and Olive gutted her place together, one room at a time. They started with the living room—nothing—and moved on to the kitchen, since it was right behind them. More nothing. Into the bedroom. Great underwear but nothing about Dust. He looked at her phone and she had his number but no messages in voicemail or text.

Into the small closet. A floor safe. "What's in there? Open it."

Olive stepped into the closet, knelt below the hanging skirts and dresses. She looked up at Rico. "There's a gun."

Rico pulled his .45 and pointed it at the floor. "Open it and step out of there. Don't reach inside."

It was a combination lock and she fumbled with the dial a few times. After a couple minutes it opened and she got out of there awkwardly but fast.

Rico aimed his pistol at her. "Sit on the bed and don't get up."

She got there in a heartbeat and sat.

Rico smiled at the pistol in the safe. A .22, a woman's weapon. He didn't touch it, didn't want his fingerprints on a weapon she looked scared enough to use. The only other thing in the safe was a jewelry box. He opened it. Nothing but jewelry, no false bottom.

"Goddamn." He shut the safe, spun the dial, and looked back at her. "Not the sentimental type, are ya? I guess Dust ain't a guy to leave things behind."

"Not things." She faced the floor. "Just people."

And now Rico figured she'd never call him. Didn't fucking matter. She'd get talked to if they wanted her.

Rico walked out of Olive's with nothing. Nothing but a desperate hope. Women who get hit either want revenge or they're too in love to do anything but protect the asshole who hit them. Olive acted somewhere in between. Maybe she didn't know anything, maybe she did without even realizing what she knew was important. But then again, she was Dust's latest girl. Maybe she knew exactly where he was, or at least how to get hold of him. Rico couldn't take the risk, not with his neck on the line. He was on his phone with Vollmer as soon as he hit sidewalk. "Send a man where I went. I want this place watched too."

There hadn't been time to plan. Just a couple hours since Dust took off with Tenny's money. Not much of a head start but Dust disappeared fast.

Already night and Rico couldn't leave here until someone he trusted was watching Olive, someone who wouldn't let her get away. She might be warning Dust already, but that didn't matter, Dust knew who was chasing him. Rico sure as hell could make sure Olive was tailed if she ran.

Rico sat in the driver's seat of his Lincoln Continental and waited. He shouldn't have to wait long, Vollmer would send someone good and nearby. Still, he hated waiting. Worst thing about any job he ever did.

His phone rang: Dietz, the guy who rented Dust his last room. Rico's guys had already gone through the room, but they couldn't talk to Dietz like Rico could. He and Dietz worked with a lot of the same people, only Dietz had a different kind of power, as much as a man can get and keep his hands clean. Rico was close enough to Tenny he didn't worry about that.

He took the call. "Yeah."

"What you look for is not where you're looking."

Dietz never said anything fast. This had to be important. "Meet at your office?"

"The house."

Fuck. Dietz lived way up in the hills. Even if Rico knew those roads better he couldn't take them fast, turns were too tight and one right after the other. "I can't leave right away. It has to be up there?"

"I will wait," Dietz said.

"I take care of somethin', then I'm there."

They both hung up. Rico called Vollmer again. "Call me if anything comes up. I'll be a while."

It was late night when Vollmer's guy got there. As soon as he did, Rico went to Dietz.

* * *

Dietz was an entrepreneur, a tall, lean man with silver hair, and properties all across the county. Like a lot of rich guys, he kept his mansion as high up in the hills as he could, like his castle might touch heaven.

The acreage around the house was bordered with an electric security fence, except the entrance at the bottom of the driveway, where armed guards manned the gate. Rico checked in with the guard in the booth, who called up to the house. After a minute on the phone, the guard slid the gate open.

Security would be tighter if Rico wasn't a friend, a man Dietz could almost trust. Even the drive inside the gate was uphill a ways, and the road curved too much for anything but a slow approach. Rico was losing time. He had good men down there in the city, but they weren't him.

He pulled up at the top of the empty drive, parked. He walked up to the porch, past the well-lit, beautifully landscaped grounds he didn't give a fuck about. Who was Dietz showing off for?

The door was wide, some fancy-as-shit wood and an old school door knocker. To its side was a standard button for a doorbell. Rico pressed it.

The man who opened the door was no butler, an obvious thug, thick and armed. Rico didn't know him but he knew the type. Knew he could take him, something to look forward to if Tenny ever went to war with Dietz. But Dietz wasn't that kind of gangster. He fought his wars with money, just had enough sense to guard it.

The thug waved him ahead and Rico walked. He kept his head turned to watch the big man. He didn't like guys behind him.

The hallway was long, paintings on the walls and a soft carpet. Rico saw it all as a waste of money, but it was Dietz's money, he could waste it how he wanted.

They reached a set of closed double doors. The thug pulled one open.

Dietz was inside. "Rico." He did some faggy wrist twirl that Rico guessed meant he should come in.

Rico pointed a thumb at the thug. "He goes first."

Dietz nodded and the thug walked away.

Rico stepped in, shut the door behind him.

The room was huge. Dietz stood not far from Rico, dressed in a black suit, white shirt, and business shoes. Dietz dressed like a banker and he was one, but some of the shit this man bankrolled had nothing to do with checking and savings accounts.

"Your office?" Rico tipped his head back, pointed past Dietz with his chin.

"This is the library," Dietz said, and gestured at the wall-to-wall bookshelves. Tall bookshelves, tall walls. Fucking books stacked to the ceiling. No one had that much time to read.

Dietz smiled. "My desk is by the window." He turned.

Rico walked with him, stopped at a giant desk, closed curtains behind it. A guy gets a house this big, Rico figured, he gets so much exercise crossing rooms he wants furniture big enough to crash on.

Rico sat down at the near side of the desk as Dietz walked around it. "What you got on Dust?"

Dietz would give Rico whatever news he had, but every bit he gave would come with a story. No sense dragging this out.

"I thought we might eat first," Dietz said, and sat in

the chair. "We could have something brought up. Not a lot of good Asian around here but I know which ones. Thai, Chinese, Indian, you know. They all deliver. But you say you have no time. Let me know if that changes. You want to talk about your friend who stayed at…" Dietz turned, pulled a file folder from behind him, set it on the desk and opened it. "Here."

Rico leaned over the desk. There were photos in the folder. "This his room?"

"After he left. My people always take pictures, in case there are questions about the security deposit. Would not have worked in my favor here. As you can see, Dust left the place pretty goddamn clean."

"He's a fucking drunk," Rico said. "He had to fuck up."

Dietz shook his head. "Not here. Always quiet, always clean. Of course, I do not know how much he was home."

"You got an idea."

"Not dates," Dietz said, "but he was seeing this barkeep. What you might call a hot little number. Never brought her here," he pointed to one of the room photos, "but your man drew attention, even when he was not with a woman. This one? Those two showed up anywhere, people with sense looked away. I am glad Dust gave me no cause to fuck with him. He messed people up for kicks."

Rico narrowed his eyes. "You knew that about Dust and didn't tell me."

Dietz shrugged. "Did not know at the time. Came up later, when you said look into it. I looked, I saw. He beat up a man for sitting next to him. Live fucking wire. Bad for business, Rick."

No one called him Rick. Just Dietz. Fucking Dietz. But the shit about Dust. Rico knew he should have kept better eyes on him, knew what the guy claimed he could do. Always thought he could trust him. "When's the last time he was seen?"

"Since you put out the…APB?" Dietz smiled. "No one has talked. It has not been that long, odds are he is gone. Or he holed up close and there is no word yet. If he is holing up, someone is going to see him."

"Then what's so urgent you called?"

"The…broads." Dietz was cultured when he had to be, when he talked to men in suits. When he talked to thugs in leather jackets and plain white T-shirts, he spoke the local language. With an accent.

"What about the broads?"

Dietz leaned on the desk, drummed his fingers on it. "As you know, there are three: Olivia, Theresa, and Valerie. You also probably know, he has fucked all three of them. What you may not know is he fucked them all recently."

Rico's eyebrows went up. "When?"

"After the mishandled bank job. You know about that, right?"

"Bank job?"

Dietz with a victory smile: "Then this is a favor to Tenny."

Rico waited for Dietz to continue, saw that Dietz waited as well. He nodded. "The word goes up."

"Good. Favors are favors."

And time is fucking money, Rico thought.

"Dust took time away from the job you got for him. You remember that much."

"Yeah yeah yeah."

"He pulled a bank job, which should come as no surprise. He fucked it up, which should. Caught a bullet, went to a doctor you know. Valerie was his ride."

Rico shrugged. "That ain't nothin'."

"He stayed with her the whole time he was out."

"That man didn't take shit when he was inside. He can sleep on a couch."

"He could. Perhaps sometimes he did." Dietz paused, always for effect. He wasn't someone who ran out of breath. "I have reason to believe that at least one time he did not."

"Reason to believe?" Rico hated answers that weren't answers.

Dietz stepped back from the desk, put his hands on his hips. "I have people who watch people."

"And what?"

Dietz smiled and his hands fell to his sides. "She kicked him out or he walked. Either way he went back and she told him to fuck off. That is a woman he cares too much about and he has known her forever. God knows what she knows."

"I already got to talk to her," Rico said.

"Meaning you did, or meaning you will?"

Rico hated when Dietz switched from semi-street to full-on professor. "I will. But it ain't no surprise. A man goes back to a woman."

"And goes back. He went back to Valerie for years, went back to Theresa the night he took the money, is bound to go back to Olivia."

"The night he took the money?" Rico leaned in, his face nearly touching Dietz's. "That's tonight."

"You are watching the front of that apartment, correct? So Dust is either still there, or went out the back."

Rico's phone was in his hand. He speed dialed Vollmer. "Go in. Careful. He might be inside."

Vollmer knew Dust owed Tenny money and took off with it. Stupid fuck. You can't run with money, and you can't leave people behind. Dust broke up with Theresa before he took off, so maybe he thought that made her safe. But Dust worked for Rico, he should've known better. Nothing's forgotten, nothing's forgiven.

So now the woman, whatever she knew. Theresa had a kid, Jeremy, and word was Dust cared about her and the boy. You owe money, somehow you pay.

At the front door of Theresa's building Vollmer pushed all the buttons but hers, like Rico taught him, waited for some fool to buzz him in. Some fool did.

Vollmer made it to the elevator unseen, pressed the up arrow. After a minute, it opened. He got in, pressed 5. The doors closed and he reached back, made sure his leather jacket hung below the holster behind him. He tugged his black T-shirt but that didn't do a damn thing, then reached for his shoulder holster, made sure it rested where he wanted. He wouldn't need either gun for the woman, but he wouldn't mind showing her one.

Vollmer leaned at her door, heard nothing inside, knocked and waited a minute. It was a weeknight and she had a kid, fucking ten o'clock, they should be home.

Vollmer wasn't here to wait. No one in the hall, he ran a credit card down the doorframe until it hit the latch, pushed himself against the door and bent the card away from the doorknob. Pushed and bent, pushed and bent. A couple minutes of that. Fuck it. He took a few steps back and ran at the door, slammed a boot hard where the strike plate should be. The door popped open and Vollmer staggered through, into the apartment. Like riding a fucking bike.

He stepped inside, shut the door behind him. A couple steps and he was taking in the kitchen with a glance. Heard movement on the far side of the apartment, couldn't tell where. He turned his head. The living room wasn't much bigger than the kitchen.

Bar stools on the living room side of the kitchen counter. Vollmer sat on one, leaned back, the elbows of his jacket on the counter. He heard a door open down the hall, slow footsteps like someone thought he wouldn't hear. He faced the hall, one ass cheek barely on the stool, waited for Theresa to step into the light.

She stepped. He saw her in the dimly lit room, green eyes in a dark face, didn't see a gun, just a nice lean shape and black hair. He got up off the stool.

"Dust?"

"That shit don't sell." Vollmer stepped toward her.

"What? Who?" She stopped halfway down the hall.

Vollmer kept walking, long strides, stood close now. "Your boy asleep somewhere?"

"You looking for Dust?"

"Where is he?"

"He left."

"I know he fucking left!" Vollmer's hand shot out fast and straight, palm open and down. His fingers jabbed into her just below the ribcage.

Theresa stepped back with a gasp, her upper body flung up like she tried to cough but couldn't. Her face went red, she had no air, then she coughed and the air came. She coughed again and stepped sideways, on one foot then the other, returned to where she'd first stepped back.

Vollmer stepped close, her open-mouthed breathing easy to hear. His face in hers, he spoke softly. "Where is he?"

"I kicked him out."

Vollmer grabbed Theresa by the hair behind her neck and yanked back hard.

"Aah!" It was a short yell, probably more surprise than pain. She stumbled, reached out with both arms for balance.

The door to the boy's room opened and Jeremy, a small boy with short black hair, ran out. "Mom!"

Vollmer pulled on Theresa's hair and she bent back farther. The boy ran at Vollmer but Vollmer put a hand out like a stop sign and Jeremy stopped. It was that or run into it. Vollmer released Theresa's hair, moved his hand to her neck. Didn't squeeze, just held her there.

"No!" Jeremy shouted.

Vollmer ignored him. "Where'd he go?"

"You ever been kicked out? You say where you fuckin' went?"

"When?"

"A-a-couple hours."

Vollmer let go of her. "I'm gonna look around. Both of you with me, every place I go. You two in front." Vollmer waved them forward.

Theresa grabbed Jeremy's hand and they started down the hall. The kid was maybe eight, maybe ten—Vollmer wasn't good on kid's ages—a lot shorter than his mom. They walked past the open bathroom door.

"Back bedroom first," Vollmer said.

Theresa walked slow enough that Jeremy's little legs could keep up. She reached the door to her bedroom—

what had been their bedroom, hers and Dust's—opened it and waited outside.

"Both of you, hands up and go in."

They raised their hands and entered slow.

Vollmer's Glock .50 was out by the time he reached the doorway. A monster of a weapon held comfortably in a massive hand. Vollmer looked all around the room, saw no one but Theresa and Jeremy, was pleased with the fear he saw on their faces. "Sit on the bed."

They did, faced each other. Vollmer swung the door open wide and pushed it hard against the wall in case Dust was there. Nothing. He looked back. Theresa and Jeremy stared at him. "Tell me where he is," Vollmer looked at Theresa, "and I won't hurt the kid."

"I told you I don't know."

Vollmer aimed his pistol at her, lowered himself to the floor and looked under the bed. No one, but there was a shoe box with a few papers in it, bills and shit like that with Dust's name on them. Vollmer stood with it and walked across the room so he could see Theresa and Jeremy on the bed while he watched the door. There was also a bathroom door, partly open. "Stay on the bed."

Vollmer crossed to the bathroom door, walked in, slid the shower curtain back and looked down into the tub. Empty, no surprise.

He returned to the bedroom, aimed his Glock at Theresa again. "Open the closet door. Just you. The kid stays on the bed."

Theresa kissed Jeremy on top of his head and got up. She got to the door and slid it open.

"Wait." Vollmer joined her, looked in. "Okay, other side."

Theresa shut the left side and Vollmer walked around

her to look in from where it would open on the right. Nothing but a woman's wardrobe, same as the left. The clothes weren't fancy but Vollmer looked at what she wore now and yeah, she'd look good in them.

"Get the kid. One more bedroom."

Theresa walked toward the bed. Jeremy joined her halfway there, took her hand. She squeezed. "We'll be alright."

"I know." Jeremy smiled but it didn't sound like he believed it.

Vollmer sneered. They walked out the door and down the hall.

"Wait," Vollmer said.

They stopped just outside Jeremy's bedroom. Vollmer walked into the half-bathroom across the hall, took a quick look, came back out. "Go." He tilted his chin toward Jeremy's room and they walked in.

"On the bed."

A quick look under the bed and Vollmer waved Theresa forward. She opened the closet without waiting for his command. A small closet with one door. Dust wasn't there.

Vollmer led Theresa and Jeremy back to the living room. "Couch." They sat, close together. Vollmer walked into the kitchen, opened the fridge, smiled at the bottles of Dos Equis. He grabbed one, set it on the counter, opened drawers until he found an opener and popped the lid off the bottle.

He took a drink, walked back to the living room and narrowed his eyes at Theresa. "You. Up."

She gave Jeremy's hand a squeeze and stood in front of Vollmer.

"On the floor. On your knees." He patted his coat

where the Glock sat in its holster. Like they'd forgotten.

Theresa stood still, except her face. It went wrong, but Vollmer couldn't say how.

"On. Your. Knees." Vollmer damn near hissed the words. "Or I kill you both."

Theresa dropped to her knees. She had to fear the worst, whatever she thought that was. Vollmer's open palm came up under her chin and tilted her head back so she faced him. Her eyes and teeth clenched.

"I go back without answers..." Vollmer shook his head. "It ain't, did you ask 'em real good? It's, where's the fucking money? Where's fucking Dust?" He moved his palm behind her neck and his thumb to her throat and squeezed. "You're gonna talk." His thumb pressed tighter.

Theresa struggled for breath, tried to shake free of Vollmer's grip.

"Mom!" Jeremy sat still.

Vollmer glared at Jeremy. "Shut. Up." His voice was a dark whisper, barely human.

The boy sat still, his mouth hanging open. Vollmer let go of Theresa's neck.

She took loud breaths, looked at Vollmer, then at Jeremy. "He—Dust—had another woman. He coulda gone to her. To them."

"Everyone knows that." Vollmer's glare was for Theresa now. "She kicked him out. Then he came back to you." It was a guess, but it was a good one, he could tell by the look on Theresa's face. "Tell me where he is."

Theresa tried to straighten, got to standing three quarters and gasped. "I—don't know."

"Tell me where he is," Vollmer whispered, bending forward so his mouth was just above her forehead, "or I kill the kid."

"God help me." Tears flowed. "He just left."

Vollmer backhanded her hard across the face. Theresa staggered back, leaned against a barstool, braced her hands on the counter behind it.

"Back we go." Vollmer waved them ahead with his gun hand. Jeremy and Theresa walked unsteady down the hall, his hand in hers. In each room Vollmer emptied the dressers a drawer at a time then shoved the dressers down. He pulled the mattresses from each bed and flipped them over on the floor, went back to each closet and checked the pocket in every piece of clothing that hung. He knocked on every wall but nothing sounded false, dumped each bathroom drawer knowing nothing was in them.

It was a small apartment and he ransacked it fast. Vollmer waved them back to the living room, took Theresa's purse and grabbed every little thing in it, looked at each, and threw them on the floor. Except her cell phone. He pocketed that.

"Okay," Vollmer said, "take off your clothes."

Theresa looked at Jeremy. "You wearin' underpants?"

Jeremy nodded, his whole body shrunk even smaller than he already was.

Theresa returned her eyes to Vollmer. She looked tired but she looked hard. "You don't touch him." She nodded in Jeremy's direction, "He takes off his jeans, that's all. I ain't strippin' either. You can frisk me."

Vollmer nodded, no expression. "You both take off your shoes. And you're gettin' frisked good."

Theresa turned to Jeremy. "Go ahead. The man won't touch you."

Jeremy bent down, undid his laces, loosened the shoes

and flipped them off his feet. They flew forward.

Vollmer checked the shoes—nothing—while Jeremy struggled to unbutton his pants.

Theresa stared at her son. "It's okay, Jeremy."

"Turn your head, mom."

She did and he got back to it, more like his usual pace. He got the jeans unbuttoned, pushed them down his legs to the floor.

Vollmer looked at Jeremy. "Toss 'em here."

He caught Jeremy's toss, went through the pockets, took a cell phone. Nothing else in them mattered.

Vollmer kicked the jeans back to Jeremy's feet, turned to Theresa. He was about to play cop. He'd been on the other end of this enough times.

"Turn and face the bar," Vollmer said. Theresa turned. "Lean on it." She did and Vollmer stepped forward, grabbed her right thigh with his right hand and yanked it back, did the same with the left. His hands moved up to just under her arms. He reached around to the front and his hands dropped to her breasts. He pulled so they pressed against her chest. He liked the way they felt but he didn't find anything. His hands dropped, groped, but this was how she wanted to do it and she didn't say a word. Vollmer felt her belly, reached down and grabbed at her crotch, brought his hands back around and grabbed her ass. Felt great but nothing he could use. He worked his way down her legs, front and back, and stepped away.

"You're clean," he said.

Vollmer took another step back, got out his wallet, grabbed a card and set it on the kitchen counter. The same card Rico handed out. "There's a number on there, can't be connected to me, but you hear from Dust, leave a message. You call the cops, or find out something and don't let me know, I come back and you watch me. I'll take care of the boy."

Theresa glared at Vollmer as he walked toward the door. "You get near Jeremy and I'll cut your balls off."

Vollmer laughed and walked out.

Rico waited to hear from Vollmer. His eyes narrowed at Dietz. "You shoulda told me he went back to Theresa's."

Dietz shrugged. "I cannot know all you do not. I assume you are a well-informed man. I thought Valerie would be the surprise."

"No one knows the shit you know. Or where you get it."

"That is why my knowledge is valuable. You had a man on Theresa's place, it made sense you would know."

Rico rubbed his eyes with thumb and middle finger. "I'm lookin' for fuckin' Dust. Anything about where he is, I need to know now. I know you're big in your circle, Dietz. You got what you call power. But Tenny got fucked on this. I ain't gettin' fucked too. Someone dies on this, it ain't me. I don't give a fuck who you are."

Dietz took a step back. He didn't have far to go. He put his hand back, touched the curtain. "Don't get stupid, Rico."

Rico was around the desk fast for a big man. One hand on Dietz's chest pushed him back to the window. "This ain't a fuckin' game, asshole. What I get's Dust. You don't get in the fuckin' way."

He dropped his hand, stepped back closer to the desk, let Dietz breathe a step away from the window. "That everything on Theresa and Valerie?"

Dietz nodded, a couple of times.

"You got anything on Olive?"

Dietz angled his head a little. "Olivia?"

"Yeah, the hot fuckin' bartender. You knew her a minute ago."

"Hard to say. She has not been at work and those two were never steady."

"And he ain't been there?"

"Christ, Rico, it has been only a few hours. How many places could he go?"

Rico's fists clenched at his sides. "One more than I know about."

Rico's phone rang. Vollmer.

"He there?" Rico asked.

"Hell no."

"Gone how long?"

"She says a couple hours. She don't say shit else. Believe what you believe, I got nothin'. Just numbers to check on her phone."

Rico ended the call, took a step toward Dietz. "Valerie's south. Any other directions Dust might go?"

"North," Dietz said. "He used to do some work for a guy in Berkeley. Or he could head east, just run. At least he cannot go west. He would be in the ocean."

"East is a waste of time, unless I get a tip. Too many places he could be. What's more likely, north or south?"

"Like I said before, he always goes back to the women."

Olivia's place was a disaster. Not a lot of stuff but all of it everywhere. Rico had thrown things around like he was desperate. No way in hell he was trying to help

Dust. He wanted to find him but why? What had Dust done? Would Rico kill him?

Not just her apartment: her life was a disaster. Because of one man and the life he'd brought her into. This hurt too much to be anything but love and it pissed her off. This was what that bullshit did. Well, Rico hadn't thrown around her glasses or bottles. She got the Maker's Mark out again. It was late, she wouldn't put on music, she'd drink in quiet. No music matched how she felt anyway. Torn, hurt, staggered, lost—hell, it was like every sad love song, only with violence and fear thrown in.

She drank, walked the apartment, looked at the knocked over furniture like she was taking inventory of the dead. Home had been a safe place, away from the madness of what was outside. She was alone now. The apartment, no longer a part of what was hers. Nothing was hers. It could all be destroyed by a stranger at any time.

She walked into the bathroom, looked in the mirror. She turned her head, looked at her beaten profile. It wasn't her. At least, it wasn't who she'd been.

She finished the glass of bourbon and poured another. She returned drawers to the dresser they'd been thrown from, returned clothes from the floor to the drawers. Only her general lack of possessions made this a task she could complete. One thing she had plenty of was booze, and she'd already had too much. She couldn't drive, so drinking and tidying were the things she'd do tonight. By morning her despair should be replaced by a hangover. Then she could deal with a different pain and whatever it was that bothered her now.

* * *

She woke up hurting. The physical pain nothing she hadn't felt before. The fear changed everything. She shook as she drank her coffee. Without the fear, she might have laughed when it spilled.

She sipped, like an old woman who should have a straw. She'd served old drinkers who needed one. Never a man with his beer, always a woman with her wine. She wondered if the men stopped going out when they couldn't drink on their own. If your drinking was a social thing, and you had to look good while you did it...She shouldn't give a fuck, not after that visit from Rico.

Olivia walked the apartment with a fresh coffee cup and a suitcase. Leave damn near everything she couldn't carry. She stuffed the suitcase full. These were her clothes, this was her life. Olivia sure as fuck did not feel like moving. And realized there was nowhere she could go.

Rico or men like him would be watching her place. And the men who watched would be better at watching than she could be at disappearing. Hell, they probably made people disappear.

Olivia set her cup on the counter, grabbed Bushmills from a cabinet and topped off the cup. Liquid courage was better than none.

She drained her juiced coffee and grabbed a bottle, dosed another coffee, and sat on the couch next to the full suitcase. Tomorrow she'd be back at work, everything the same, except her face was half wrecked. By that prick, the man she'd thought loved her. Where the pain kicked in now, on top of the fear—that goddamn glass he slammed against her cheek meant he cared more than she thought.

Olivia threw the full suitcase as far as she could. It plopped down short of the living room wall. She drank. The man who maybe loved her wasn't coming back. The men who chased him might be. She hoped Dust got away. She'd seen what Dust could become, but Rico might be worse.

Taking the coast would be a beautiful drive, but Rico wasn't adding time to this. He drove ugly freeways with his windows up. Inland, even with traffic, was faster.

Rico knew a little about Valerie, wondered a lot. Why was Dust still tight with a teenage girlfriend? She was probably obsessed, a crazy occasional hot fuck. Rico looked forward to seeing what she looked like. Dust hadn't said a goddamn word about her.

Rico couldn't trust anything she'd say. Like with anyone, but especially someone's woman. Problem was, almost everyone who knew Dust was one of his women. Not that he'd have said much to them either, but he drank, words could slip out.

The inside of the car heated up. Tired already, he turned on the AC and drank from the large coffee he'd bought on his way out of Oakland. It wasn't great but it helped. He flipped his leather jacket open on the passenger seat, enough to reach the inside pocket and grab the plastic baggie. He took a hand off the wheel, opened the bag, grabbed three black beauties and popped them, washed them down with a slug of coffee.

He was only halfway to Valerie's, should be alert as hell by the time he got there. He wondered what Valerie was like. That Olive, he could get into that, and he'd heard Theresa wasn't bad either. Val, that's what Dust liked to call her when the mood was right.

He got off the freeway and pulled over, flipped open his street map. He liked driving but not GPS. Didn't like cell phones or computers either. Too many fucking things getting between him and the world. Too much time in a car on the freeway, too much time talking to and about Dust's pretty women without fucking them. Rico was ready to burst. He'd control himself when he talked to Valerie, but maybe after…

He saw the streets he needed on the map and pulled away from the curb. He'd taken the right off-ramp, had about a mile to go. He knew where he should turn, took it slow so he didn't overshoot it. Damn small towns, any alley could be the street he needed. He got honked at a couple times, flipped off a couple kids. Fucking punks. Rico didn't pull stupid shit like busting people up over shit like that but he felt like it every time.

He saw the street, turned, drove slow enough to read addresses. Close to where he wanted, he found a place to park on the street and pulled over. All the houses had driveways and mailboxes on the edge of the street. Rico saw the number he wanted. A Volvo in the driveway. The plates checked.

Rico walked up the driveway, knocked on Valerie's door. He saw the bell, pressed it, heard nothing. Knocked again.

"A minute!" A holler from inside, a strong female voice. This might be interesting. He waited. A full minute, then some more. The doorknob turned and the door opened a crack.

A pistol barrel showed in the gap. "Step back!"

Rico stepped.

The pistol aimed at his chest. "You ain't Dust?" The voice wasn't so strong now, but deep for a woman. "Who the fuck are ya?"

"A friend. Worried about him. What he could do."

"Put your coat on the porch. Turn out your pants pockets."

Rico shook his head. "You're outta your fucking mind."

"Right. And I'll put six in your chest. This is a .45. You won't be gettin' up."

"I wear a shoulder holster," Rico said. "Don't panic when you see it. I take my pistol out by the barrel and lay it on the porch. Then I drop the coat on top."

"Alright," she said. "No tricks."

Rico shook his head again, hoped she could see that. He held out thumb and forefinger, brought them slowly to the pistol in the shoulder holster. He faced the gun barrel in the doorway, squatted, put his pistol down and took his jacket off one sleeve at a time without turning, made sure not to show the pistol in the holster behind his back.

"Come in. Shut the door behind you. I'm willing to kill you inside too."

Rico didn't know what Dust had done to this woman. He had to find out. He stepped in, shut the door. She was huge. "You Valerie?"

"Does it matter?"

"I came to talk to Valerie." Rico was barely inside the doorway. She stood a few feet in front of him, in the spare space that passed for a living room.

"Why?"

"Dust tell you he quit drinking a few months back? Prob'ly not. When he fell off the wagon, he fell hard."

"He was drinking last I saw him." She held the big pistol in one hand, a goddamn Colt .45.

Rico didn't like how comfortable it looked in her hand. From this range that would kill him fine. "You wanna lower that? I'd hate to get killed by accident, Val."

"Yeah, I'm Val." She lowered her .45 slowly, stopped when it aimed at the floor.

Rico brought his hand from behind his back and aimed the Glock at her head. "Lay your fucking gun on the floor." He hated to be disarmed. Hadn't happened in years.

Val set her pistol down. "That's fucked up."

"Tell me where Dust is or you find out what fucked up means."

"What the hell you think you gonna do? What you think you gonna take from me? Fuck you."

Rico's Glock was aimed at her head and she didn't give a fuck. Now Rico knew whose rapist Dust killed in prison. It was just a story before, now it was Valerie. The woman who'd been raped, her children murdered in front of her. It was there in Val's eyes—she'd already lost everything.

"Okay," he said. "We do this another way. Put the gun down first though."

She looked at the barrel of the Glock, looked Rico in the eyes. She placed the Colt on the carpet.

He waited until she stood with her pistol out of reach. "Buy you a drink?"

"I ain't goin' out. Jameson alright?"

"Pour me one. Keep the bottle out." Rico watched her walk to the kitchen, grab a bottle and two glasses and take a seat on the living room couch. He holstered his Glock and sat beside her. The two of them filled the couch. She leaned forward, poured the glasses tall. Not the usual way he got information, but if he had to fuck this big bitch Rico was gonna enjoy it.

Val took a hearty slug, set her glass down. "He ain't here."

Rico glanced at her, kept drinking.

"It's a small place," she said. "Pretty obvious he wouldn't fit."

"He try to fit?" Rico finished his glass, poured another.

She grinned. "He ain't much at tryin'. He just does shit."

"He threaten you?"

Val held the bottle. "Dust? Threaten me? Worst thing he could do is stay."

"He done worse. To others. Must like you." Rico took the bottle from her, filled her glass and set down the bottle. "Glad he likes you." He drank.

"Why?" Her turn to drink.

"You two didn't end good?"

"End was okay," she said. "It's what came before."

"Way he leaves, some got no regrets he's gone."

"I miss...someone," Val said. "Been a long time since that's who he was."

"Yeah? Who was he?"

"He used to take care of me. I don't need that any-more."

"Whaddaya need now?"

She drank. "This." She set the glass down. "And men without guns."

"You said he didn't threaten you."

"It's the way he lived, how he thought. He didn't give a fuck about people." She shrugged, a rise and fall of heavy shoulders. "I used to be his girl. Now he thinks I'm his pet."

Rico topped off her glass, drank from his own. "You don't look like no pet."

"No? What do I look like?"

"A woman. Alone."

She pulled her head back. Her body had nowhere to go. "That a threat?"

"I don't hurt women." It was a lie. Rico hurt anyone who got in his way. But Val wasn't in his way yet. She might have the money, might know where Dust was. He'd find out.

She was quiet a minute, like Rico's words were complicated. "Be nice," she said, "to find a guy who doesn't hurt anyone."

"Everyone hurts someone."

"Yeah." Val drank. "Some do it like it's second nature."

"You know I work with Dust and you're tellin' me this."

"Why's that matter to you? Thought you were lookin' for money."

"Work ain't all I do." Rico took a short drink. "You're damn pretty, Val."

It was true, and maybe it was what she wanted to hear.

Her eyes narrowed, like he might be playing her, then looked into her glass. "Work's what you're doin' now."

"Dust is my friend." Rico drank again. "He hurts people he cares about, that ain't him. Him when he's drinkin'—that ain't him."

"Dust always drank. At least since high school."

"Yeah, but he ain't always a prick about it. I knew

him inside. Didn't drink much there. And there was a guy in there. You know what happened, right? He did that for you. He tell you he'd do that?"

Her eyes went wide and blinked, like she wanted a veil over her face to hide the pain. Rico was talking about Peach, the man who'd raped her and killed her boys in front of her. And he was telling her what she should have already known, that Peach dying in the same prison where Dust was also doing time...she had to already know it wasn't coincidence, but she didn't think about the revenge Dust got for her, she only saw that monster with his hands on her boys, then those same hands on her. She shook her head, grabbed her glass and gulped down the end of it.

"Dust took care of you," Rico said. "But he wasn't right for you. I just wanna find him."

She blinked rapidly, looked at Rico. "I don't wanna talk about this."

"I just gotta find him. Find the man, turn in the money. Before anyone else gets hurt."

Her eyes narrowed as she glared. "That a threat?"

"A reminder," Rico said. "I'm still workin', but I got a personal interest."

"In him." She poured herself another glass of Jameson.

He switched drinking hands, put an arm around Val.

She shrugged. "I don't need comforting."

His arm held tighter. "Ain't why I'm here."

"No," she said. "You're here for him."

"Lookin' for him." Rico ran thick fingers through her hair. "Let's see where I look."

He kissed her. After a moment, she kissed back.

* * *

Rico had expected Val to be pretty, and she was. He hadn't expected her to be fat and fearless. He was alright with all of that as he lay in bed with her, but she'd fallen asleep, hadn't talked yet. And he didn't want to keep Carelli waiting.

He had to wake her up. He rolled back on top of her, kissed the rolls of her neck, then her massive breasts. Her hand grabbed his dick but it remained limp.

"That don't feel like you."

"I gotta go," Rico said. "I'll come back, and I'll feel like that again. But I wanted to kiss you goodbye." He lowered his mouth to her massive belly.

Val moaned, put both hands on top of Rico's head and pushed down.

Rico went down all the way, Val's vast body spread around and above him. He liked this, he stayed there. After several minutes, he was hard and he came up.

"Condom!" Valerie said.

"We're dyin' young." Rico plunged his dick inside her and they fucked like it had been weeks, not an hour. He pulled out and came on her belly. She brought her hand down and rubbed it around on herself.

Rico lay on top of her. He was ugly, she was fat, and they were together. The last part of that was about to end. "Val, this ain't why I'm here, but I really like you."

Val pushed herself up with her palms. "But what?"

"Nothing. Just, I gotta go, I'm supposed to find Dust. And if I don't, they're after me."

"After? Like a hit?"

Rico shook his head. "I'll be in trouble. I don't think they'll kill me."

"They'll kill Dust, though. Is that it?"

"Dust took some money." Rico rolled on his side,

propped himself up with an elbow and faced her. "They want the money."

"Then they forgive him. Is that it?"

"I know Dust a long time. I get the money and Dust gets away, I'm okay with that."

Val grabbed a pillow and propped herself up better. "You think I know about the money?"

"The money, Dust, anything you know helps."

Val's hand came up fast, smacked hard against Rico's cheek. "Fuck you, Rico. I thought you liked me."

Rico grinned, thin and evil. "I don't kill you for that, Val. That's how much I like you. I gotta know about Dust is all, so they don't come after me. Tell me what you know, I finish my business, I come back and see you."

"I don't know shit. Ain't seen that bastard since I kicked him out of here."

"Gotta search the joint."

"Like hell."

"It ain't a request."

"Do what you fucking want but don't expect any help. And don't leave a mess."

Rico got up, dressed, dumped everything he saw on the ground, tore the place to fucking pieces like gutting a corpse. Didn't find a goddamn thing he could use.

Val got out of bed naked, walked to the kitchen and poured herself a fresh Jameson. "Don't matter what you say, you ain't comin' back."

Rico looked through everything, even photo albums where he saw a lot of pictures of a guy who must've been Dust a lot of years ago. Nothing else about him. Rico left, Val still in the kitchen, naked and drinking.

* * *

Olivia woke, if you could call it that. Already mid-afternoon and she had to shower and come out of the bathroom looking good. As good as she could look with the scar. Which would fuck with her tips and maybe bring in some freaks. Goddamn Dust.

And there could be worse than freaks. Rico acted like he'd be back to see her soon. She didn't know what that meant. She'd told him the truth and there was nothing else to remember. Unless he found Dust he was coming back.

She crossed the apartment to her bedroom closet in a hurry, splashed coffee on the carpet. She didn't slow down, knelt inside the closet and set her near empty cup on top of the safe. She spun the dial a few times to the right, slowed down and stopped at 86. Then left past 24 once, twice, and stop the third time. Back to the right, past 17 once, stop the second time, turn it back to the left and wait to feel the click. Nothing. Fuck. Spin right a few times again, start over. A sip of coffee before dialing this time.

Third try she got it, on edge by now, didn't look as she reached inside and grabbed the pistol. It was always loaded when she put it away but she checked. Yep. She shut the safe and spun the dial left, made sure it was locked. Jewelry in there, inherited or given by men she didn't want to remember, better than the stuff she'd bought for herself. The shit she bought herself was in drawers Rico dumped and she'd refilled.

Olivia sat on her knees, pistol tight in one hand. She grabbed her coffee cup in the other and stood. No fingers near the trigger, barrel down. She'd practiced at the range a lot but never for anything like this. She put the pistol in her purse and finished her coffee, stood there a minute with an empty cup, but she was as easy to find here as there and if she stayed here her thoughts wouldn't be interrupted. She needed the interruptions.

The Big Wheel didn't open until five, so Olivia didn't have to be greeted by another bartender, which was good; she wouldn't have to deal with much sympathy for her face. She'd get some from the Mexican guys in the kitchen, and whoever was on tables tonight. No other bartenders this shift and those were the guys who'd be over the top. One of the advantages of this place, fewer coworkers meant less camaraderie.

She got there at 4:30, locked the door behind her and checked how much prep work she had to do. The usual, lemons and limes. Didn't look like they were out of or low on anything that mattered, so no last-minute runs to the store across the street. She grabbed a glass and poured a couple fingers of Maker's Mark. Her first night back and her face like this, it was gonna be weird, might as well ease her way into it.

One more thing. Had to have the pistol in easy reach. She put it under the bar in front.

A knock at the door, a Mexican voice. Alejandro, a real nice guy and of course he said something as soon as she let him in. "Oh, your face, are you okay?"

"Nothing that matters," she said. "Nothing I wanna talk about."

He smiled and walked past her. The best worker in the kitchen got here early so he could start prepping, not talk. When the other Mexicans got here he'd be talking all night, sometimes holler something funny to her in English. Especially on a slow night, and it was early enough in the week this might be one.

Olivia shut the door behind him, didn't lock it. The rest of the crew should be here soon. She had bourbon to drink and fruit to slice. She got behind the bar again and threw back a shot, grabbed a handful of limes and a knife and started cutting. She finished with the limes, dropped them in a mug and set it under the bar, raised her glass as the door opened. Felipe walked in and held the door for Jeanie, their star waitress, a sweet young thing and cute as a fucking button, seemed far too Iowa to work in a South Bay bar.

Jeanie thanked Felipe, caught a glance of Olivia's face and ran to her. "Olivia, what happened? It was that Dust, wasn't it?"

Olivia finished her drink and shook her head. "I got it handled. He's gone. It's fine."

"What did he hit you with? You poor thing."

The only coworker tonight where Olivia had to worry about this kind of shit. "It was an accident. We broke up anyway. He ain't comin' back."

"You sure you're alright? You wanna talk about it?"

Fuck, this was worse than getting hit. "I got work to do. Go fold napkins."

Jeanie got a hurt look on her face before she walked away. It was her own goddamn fault. Jesus, grow up. Olivia poured herself some more Maker's and grabbed a bunch of lemons and a different knife. A drink, then a lot of slicing and another tall mug for the lemons. She finished the lemons as the rest of the staff rolled in.

It was five minutes 'til but Olivia was ready to start making tips. She pulled the door all the way open so it clicked into place against the wall and returned to her spot behind the bar, finished her second glass and waited for the assholes.

They weren't all assholes, thankfully, but almost every man who sat down wanted her and she knew it in an instant. She figured that was tip money, she couldn't drive them away. Still, she'd dressed a little warmer than necessary tonight, the opposite of her usual strategy. And they wouldn't all want her the way she looked now.

She was scrolling through Facebook on her phone when Jerry, a nice guy who worked up the street, came in and sat down at the middle of the bar.

"Oh, hey," he said, in a tone that had to mean concerned.

Olivia figured she'd get a lot of that tone tonight. "Lagunitas?"

"Yeah. Thanks."

She knew he had a lot of questions. What? How? Why? Who? But Jerry wasn't the type to pry. He sat there, questions unasked. None of them mattered. It was done, Dust was gone. Short of death, you couldn't have much more finality than that.

Still, it threw her. Dust drank the whole time she knew him, but he was never that kind of prick before. He tried to be good to her but something was eating him. And he was good, until he drank too much. Toward the end, he always drank too much.

She gave Jerry his drink—she didn't say his name, cardinal sin in tip collecting—and returned to the end of the bar nearest the door and poured herself another drink, more of the same.

Timothy walked in, a fat man who always sat alone at a table, rarely talked to anyone but his waitress. This time he had someone with him. Behind him so Olivia couldn't quite see, a smaller man lurking in the fat man's shadow.

"The guy you're lookin' for?" Timothy said. "He knows Olivia," he nodded in her direction, "but she don't say shit."

Ah fuck. Timothy rolled in her direction. It was a big roll, four hundred pounds easy, the man behind him still out of sight. "Honey." His voice deep like something from the gutter. "Where's Dust?"

"I don't know," and Olivia had an arm out with a pistol aimed at the motherfucker's head.

"Heyyyy," Timothy said, "it's only a question."

"Rico send you?"

"He couldn't make it, said I should check on you."

"I'm fine." Olivia held the pistol steady. "Go."

"Honey, I'm goin', but better for you, you talk to me now."

"Better for you, walk outta here still breathin'."

It was only a .22. Olivia didn't know if it would kill a man that size, but if she took one shot she'd keep shooting until she found out.

Timothy watched Olivia's eyes, opened his mouth and said nothing. He took a step back, then another, backward to the door, his friend, if he existed, already outside. Timothy's eyes were narrow slits, like he'd faced pistols before and wasn't gonna let one stare him down. He barely fit through the doorway on his way out.

Jerry waited a few seconds, like the big man might return. "You gonna call the cops? He might not be far away."

"I pulled the gun," Olivia said, but she'd already thought about where the fat man would go. Where he'd wait for her.

* * *

The rest of Olivia's shift was a mess. She couldn't focus on anything except she'd pulled a gun on a man who looked like he might kill her. She knew she was out of her league. She mixed up tickets, screwed up drink orders, ignored customers who talked to her at the bar. Fuck me, she thought. That man might kill me.

An hour before closing, her phone was in her hand and she called a number that had rarely called hers, a number she'd have deleted if she'd thought about it. It went straight to voice mail.

"There's a man outside the bar. He's looking for you. I pulled a gun on him. I think he might kill me. I'm sure he's going to hurt me."

Olivia didn't know if Dust still had the same phone, if he checked messages, if he'd come back and put his own life at risk. God, that was probably the whole plan. She redialed, got voice mail again.

"Don't come. You're the one he wants to kill. Prick."

The Big Wheel made it through the night without any cop visits about the gun. The guy Olivia pulled it on wouldn't call, the staff was all on her side, even that little bitch Jeanie (and she wasn't a bitch, she was the opposite so Olivia didn't relate), and Jerry had been the only customer at the time and he liked her. It was past 12 and most of the staff were gone. Only Alejandro was still in the kitchen. He usually got out faster than this on a slow night.

The bar was empty. Olivia was done with her shift, money in the safe and the place was clean, handwritten notes about what they needed—booze and mixers, they bought fresh fruit every day—taped to the register. She needed Alejandro to leave and she needed to leave after that, but she hadn't come up with a plan for leaving other than keeping her pistol where she could reach it.

"Olivia." Alejandro always pronounced her name musically, like she was beautiful no matter how she felt. It didn't make her feel safe. She didn't know if anything would.

She turned to him as he stepped beside her. "You ready to go?"

"You're worried tonight. I walk you to your car."

Olivia didn't think she was capable of a smile. "Thanks." She wanted to say more but she couldn't start talking, didn't know when she'd stop.

Didn't know if she felt safer with Alejandro beside her. At least she wasn't alone. She didn't want to endanger him, but she knew him—if anything happened to her it would eat him up. Better than being dead, but Timothy had no reason to kill. He wanted information about Dust.

The walk to her car was dark.

"Alejandro, we're gonna get jumped."

Alejandro kept pace with Olivia's fast steps. "We'll fight."

"That guy's a killer."

"Walk in the street." He stepped off the curb.

Olivia joined him. They faced traffic as they walked, could get back on the sidewalk if they had to, but there weren't many cars. She looked at Alejandro. "My life isn't like this."

"Remember Iguala?"

"Iguala?"

"Forty-three Mexican students murdered."

Olivia nodded. "God yeah."

"Life is like this."

Olivia watched for the fat man. Her hand clutched at her pistol in the purse that hung from her shoulder. Found it, gripped the handle.

Alejandro looked at her. "Don't touch the trigger."

"You can tell?"

She heard a footstep behind her, then a voice.

"Drop the purse. Don't turn around."

Olivia was sure she'd recognize the fat man's voice. This was different, reedy. A mugging? She stopped. "Are you going to kill me?"

"We gonna talk. Your friend gonna leave."

Alejandro turned his head to face the man. "I ain't—"

The man's pistol slammed into Alejandro's forehead and he fell to his knees.

Olivia turned around, her hand still in her purse. "Don't hurt him."

The man swung again, hard across Olivia's temple and she was on her side, clinging to consciousness like she might never wake.

Alejandro scrambled toward the man's feet and a boot kicked him between two ribs. Alejandro lay face down next to the curb, gasped for breath while the man knelt down and lifted Olivia in his arms, carried her away like a hero. She passed out.

ACT 3

Olivia woke up seated in a moving car, blindfolded. Her head throbbed. She didn't know if she should talk, or could. She opened her mouth and it hurt. She shut it without speaking. Under the blindfold, tears welled. "I can't cry."

Someone laughed. It sounded too high to be real.

Olivia returned to the question she'd had in her head before the pain kicked in. "Where are we going?"

"Where's Dust?" It was the reedy voice.

"Who's here?"

Like whoever it was would answer that. Whoever he was, she bet he knew how to use a gun.

No answer, and no other questions: she was left alone. With her pain and her thoughts and the water in her eyes.

Rico kept driving. Late night and the roads were empty. Fit how he felt. Too late to find Carelli. Never surprise a dangerous man at night unless you're killing him. So he'd get in late but not too late, hoped there was a place to get a drink or two near the airport. Only area where he trusted the hotels. They had to have something decent, for businessmen and pro athletes. Not everyone who went to Oakland went to kill a man or shake him down. Not everyone.

The drive to Oakland was easy enough. Getting anything from Carelli would be a different matter. Not a man Rico could threaten easily. Too much muscle behind him.

Traffic picked up after Rico got on the 880, slowed to under the speed limit at Fremont. Traffic's for men with time. Rico had some tonight. He was almost to Hayward, get past there and he'd be just outside of East Oakland. There was a Hilton Hotel on Hegenberger. Rico trusted the Hilton. Crackheads wouldn't stagger in and accidentally shoot up the wrong room.

Rico liked a quiet car, but there was too much in his head. He turned on the radio. Station after station, crackling reception or new shit he hated. Him and the radio, going nowhere.

Right now, he hated everything between him and Dust. He wanted the money, he wanted the man, he wanted to be the one who found him. Cross me, ya fuck. See who dies next. It ain't you. It's whoever's left you love.

He got past Hayward and traffic cleared. San Lorenzo, San Leandro, Oakland. Rico got off at Hegenberger, found the Hilton.

The man at the counter was a twig in a suit.

"Where's a bottle?" Rico asked. On his own turf he'd have asked for a girl. He'd already have the bottle.

Twigman blinked. "The hotel bar is closed now."

Rico grinned ugly. He wasn't the usual late night traveler. "Didn't ask that. Where do I get a bottle?"

It took a couple extra syllables to get there, but Twig-in-a-suit told Rico what he wanted to know. Rico didn't thank him, shook his head and walked away. Class joints like the Hilton were safe, but sleazy places, you buy a bottle from the guy at the counter and maybe a girl too. Always money to be made behind the counter. Some guys don't know it.

Rico knew that much and then some. Knew there was an East Bay war between Keene and Lee, knew better than to get in the middle of it. Keene and Lee were bosses anyway, not sources of information. They were the last people who'd say a word, even if he could get in a room with one of them.

Carelli traded information. Independent of the gangs, he benefited from both, didn't take sides. He was protected by his own private soldiers, but it didn't come up much.

Keene and Lee were bigger than Tenny. Rico wouldn't fuck with them if he didn't have to. If Dust was in the East Bay, he might have to. He owed Tenny. Paying him back was the only thing that might save his life.

Vollmer rolled his window down, let some air in to make the wait more comfortable. He checked his pistol, pulled it quick—it felt good in his hand—and returned it to its holster. Smooth, easy, heavy, lethal. Show up, prick.

Theresa's car was parked out front. It didn't make sense for Dust to risk coming back, but he robbed Tenny and that didn't make sense. If Dust came for the girl and they slipped out the rear exit, Vollmer wouldn't see them. But if she left in her own car, he'd see her. He had to wait where he was.

Half an hour later, Stone called. He was out back. Good.

The stakeout wasn't planned. Vollmer got a call and showed up and he might be here all night. All because one fucking idiot wanted Tenny's money. Wanted to die was more like it. Vollmer wanted action. All he got was time.

That Theresa, though, she'd be a nice prize. Only he wouldn't get her. Jobs didn't go that way. Idiots went for the pussy, led to jail time or worse. Jealous men with guns was one thing, women who got something on you was worse. Vollmer knew too much about that one.

Okay, he wouldn't touch the broad. That mother-fucker Dust, though...

Vollmer's head ran wild with shit he wouldn't do—Theresa naked in his hands, him in her even if she hated it—Dust in his sights, whoever he was whatever he looked like. Head shot, gut shot, and a couple extra as the bastard went down. Vollmer smiled. This wait would be a real letdown if none of that came true.

It was late when the building door opened and a woman came out, a suitcase in each hand. The night was dark but that was her. Theresa walked to her car, opened the trunk, put the suitcases in, looked over each shoulder. Vollmer slunk down as she slammed the trunk shut and returned to the building fast.

Vollmer called Rico. "She's making her move."

"Alone or with help?" Rico didn't sound surprised.

"With bags. I'll call back when she's on the road."

Rico hung up first and fast. Like he had something too. What was none of Vollmer's business, but he wondered. Glad Stone was out back. Suitcases in a car could be a decoy. Dust might come round back and grab the broad and the kid. Stone was under orders to follow and call. If Vollmer chased he was authorized to improvise. No secret what that meant.

Only a few minutes and Theresa came out again. She walked fast, Jeremy in one hand, travel bag in the other. She threw the bag in the back seat while Jeremy got in front.

Vollmer called Stone. "She's leaving. I got her. Stay on the back. Call me if he shows. And stay with him. But careful."

Careful wasn't the best way to describe Stone, and there's times a fearless man needs a warning. Rico said Dust was dangerous and when Rico said that it meant something. God knows who this motherfucker killed or how.

It was morning, not yet rush hour. Vollmer started the car.

Theresa's place was a couple miles to the freeway. Vollmer phoned Rico. "Just her and the kid, getting on the freeway. Heading north."

"Me, too," Rico said. "Gotta see Carelli."

"Oakland?"

"Yeah. Talk to the girl, let me know."

"Carelli's connected heavy."

Rico shrugged. "Who ain't?"

Like Rico, Vollmer headed north. If Theresa went to the Bay Area, could mean Oakland, could mean San Francisco. Vollmer liked San Francisco. Lotta nasty shit if you knew where to drop your dollars. East Bay was okay too, but those girls were harder to scare, grew up getting fucked by men with guns.

***

"Where are we going, mom?" Jeremy was ten years old but small for his age, sounded as young as he looked. "Are we running from that man?"

"He thinks we know where Dust is. I'm trying to find out."

Jeremy had been pressed against the passenger side door. Now he leaned toward his mom. "But you said you don't know where to look."

"Did that man seem like he'd help us or Dust?"

"He scared me," Jeremy said. "I meant it when I tried to hit him."

"Not the sort of man we want surprising us again, right?"

"But," Jeremy said, "you said you're trying to find Uncle Dust. If we find him, will you tell that man where he is?"

Theresa kept her eyes on the freeway traffic. "We're going to Berkeley. Dust knows a man there. He might be able to help us all."

Jeremy said, "A man? Who?"

"I don't know him personally." Theresa was glad she had to keep her eyes on the road and not on Jeremy. "I know who he is. I know where he lives."

"Who is he?"

"Uncle Dust used to work for him."

"What kind of work?" Jeremy asked.

"The kind of work Dust does," Theresa said.

"That's not an answer."

"His name is Keene," Theresa said. "I know where he lives."

"Does Uncle Dust do bad things?" Jeremy asked. "That's what I think. That's why you won't tell me."

"He does things he shouldn't. I don't know how bad

they are."

"You don't know what he does? Then how do you know he shouldn't?"

"He said," Theresa swallowed, changed lanes to get around a slow truck, got well ahead of it and cut back over, "he said we were safer if we didn't know."

"Are we running away because it's safer?"

"We aren't running away. We're going to a man who might know where Dust is."

"So..." Jeremy hesitated. "We're doing what's safe?"

"Your whole life, Jeremy, I've protected you. I do what I think's best for us. We've done okay so far, right?"

"If we find Uncle Dust, he'll protect us."

"We might need to help him, too," Theresa said. "That's what families do."

"I wish Uncle Dust was never an asshole."

Theresa's voice dropped. "He made mistakes. Somewhere, I bet he's still making them."

"But we want to find out where."

"Yes," she said. We might need to, she thought.

Theresa had an address for Keene. She didn't know if the address was where Keene lived or just a place where Dust met him once. She'd found the note crumpled at the back of a clothes drawer Dust had used. The address stuck in her head: 2731 Hunter. She'd wanted to forget and flush it down the toilet. But when that man came looking for Dust, the address came back to her and wouldn't leave.

She knew Dust was a criminal, assumed Keene would be too. Someone Dust once drunkenly told her he'd worked for. The kind of man who could tell Dust what to do. It didn't seem likely that he'd help, but it was the only card Theresa had.

* * *

Vollmer stayed close. Theresa was scared, that was good. Scared for the kid, scared for herself. She probably knew where Dust was, at least had a good idea. Why didn't he take her with him? Dust was fucked anyway if he went to Oakland. Rico was already there talking to Carelli. She finds Dust under those circumstances, it won't be a sentimental reunion.

Vollmer wanted to be there for that.

Halfway to Oakland, Vollmer heard his phone. Rico. He picked up. "Yeah."

"I need more guys on this. Everyone good, they call me."

"You need 'em there?"

"I need 'em to call me. You on your way?"

"Yeah."

"Call them first. Call me when you get here. And when she stops." Rico hung up.

Vollmer didn't like getting treated like a pest, but Rico always kept it short. If Rico was on edge, Tenny was on him. Bad time to go at the man. Not that there was a good time. Vollmer didn't scare, but he wouldn't let his temper make him stupid. He was following this woman, he wasn't walking into hell.

Whoever let Theresa and Jeremy into the house barely opened the door. Their bags were still in the car. Like this wasn't the place she'd stay, and she wasn't leaving the car behind. Houses behind houses here, so no rear exit and no way they'd try to escape on foot. Only thing around here besides houses was a corner store a couple blocks back. Nowhere to duck into.

Vollmer sat in his car across the street from the house, wondered why Rico went to Oakland when Theresa went to Berkeley.

Maybe Rico was getting backup. Vollmer wasn't charging in anyway. Dust was a dead man, now or later. Let him step out in the open and pick him off like a snake.

Vollmer kept checking his rearview, for cops or anyone else, didn't get out of the car for no one.

Olivia woke. She wasn't in a car anymore, that much had changed. A wooden chair forced her back into an awkward position and poked at her thighs just beneath her ass. It felt like an elementary school chair. Her head throbbed.

The same reedy voice from the car, the one she didn't know: "Tell me where Dust is. Or I wait with you. I think he'll come to you—thanks for that message you left on his phone—but I'll ask until you answer."

Her eyelids flipped up but not far—still blindfolded. She wanted to see him, the man whose vague threat carved possibilities she didn't want to imagine.

"I told you." She was weak, tired. "He left."

"Where?"

He slapped her across the cheek, not hard but every new pain made her take an extra breath, and her head hurt so bad her breaths became a wheeze, a rapid open-mouthed thing that hurt her throat as well. "I," and tears welled again. Her face hurt so much she'd forgotten her wet cheeks. "I..." She coughed and it turned into a fit, a thing beyond her control that knocked her head front to back and sometimes to the side and every movement hurt more.

"Where?" He slapped her across the other cheek.

Olivia tipped her head back so she faced the ceiling, although she couldn't see it, and screamed.

Hands gripped her shoulders and shook her. "Calm down."

She kept screaming, unable to see and needing to. Her neck convulsed.

His hands came up from her shoulders and held her head like a vise, stopped the violent back and forth of her head. "Slow. Down. Talk."

Tears made it out from under her blindfold, tapped his thumbs. She gasped, continually, no words, just tears.

"Where. Is. He. Or I hit you again."

She screamed so loud and high pitched that he let go of her. She felt him step back and tried to stand in her chair. It didn't rise with her; she raised herself a hair and dropped back into it. Her scream stopped and she started again.

This slap sent her and the chair to the ground. She heard a crack and she grunted and hoped the crack was the chair, not her. She opened her mouth again but her breath was gone. Tried to force a sound but nothing came. She lay on a carpet except where the chair came between it and her. She wanted to look up, see what asshole hit her this time. She wanted to see anything. The blindfold pissed her off. Her pants were wet.

No one had talked in a while. She lay there, assumed she was still being watched. As close to a snarl as she could muster: "Asshole."

It came out a wisp.

"Look," he said. "You don't owe this guy nothin'.

He beat you. Tell me where he is."

"Or you'll beat me? So I owe you nothin' too."

"Or I won't." He hit a real high, scratchy note on that one. "Make that deal with yourself."

Olivia shook her aching head, stopped fast, gave the pain a second to pause. "The one he left me for. That's all I know. He isn't comin' back to me."

"He told you?"

Olivia lay on her side on the floor, took a minute, caught breath again. "Men don't tell. Not men like that."

"What's her name?"

"You know." Barely strong enough to speak. "I don't."

"You protect her too?"

Olivia quivered. "I can't." Her voice cracked. "Even protect me."

"No one protects no one. You play that way too, you'll be alright."

Olivia cried like she had dry heaves, unable to move more than the chair would allow, unable to drench the ground, only the blindfold. On the verge of passing out again.

"If he left you," the man said, "he left you to die."

Olivia woke, tied to a heavier chair, felt like a recliner. It was positioned straight up so that's how she sat.

"He left you to die," the reedy voice said again.

"He hit me with a glass first." The words barely made it out of her mouth.

"You should have another."

Olivia's head jerked back.

Even his laugh was reedy. She recognized it as his this

time, not like in the car when it seemed unreal.

He placed a plastic cup in her hand, pushed her fingers around it. "Water. For your throat."

"What's in it?" she rasped. "Truth serum?"

"Don't matter to you, you're already tellin' the truth. Right?"

Olivia's mouth was parched. Pain all over. She took a sip from the cup. Tasted like water. She drank it all.

He took the empty cup from her, stepped away. A minute later it was in her hand again.

She took a small drink. "How long do I stay here? With you."

"Less time if you talk."

"But I told the truth. So we're here forever?"

Maybe he shrugged. Whatever he did, Olivia didn't hear. She didn't like the blindfold, being shut out. "So I never see you?"

"No. But you don't talk, you'll feel me."

"Christ," Olivia said, "you hurt me enough."

"Not what I meant. You're a beautiful woman. Despite your scar. You'll feel me."

Olivia lay on a bed blindfolded, her hands tied behind her. Her clothes were still on but she didn't know how long that would last. Didn't know if it mattered much how this asshole touched her. It was going to hurt and she was going to hate it.

A freshly lit cigarette added to the residue that hung in the room.

"We in a Motel 6 or what?"

"Better you don't know where we are," the voice said.

"Or who you are, or anything but shit I don't know

about Dust. I hate that motherfucker. I'd tell you where he was if I knew."

"Women who hate motherfuckers? I seen 'em go back to 'em."

"Not me," Olivia said. "I been hit enough."

"Maybe. But you called him."

The blindfold made it like he was invisible, a ghost.

"I," her voice cracked. "Was desperate. I thought he might save me."

The ghost laughed, thin clicks of sound. "You thought he felt guilty?"

"I. Hoped."

"That dick takes and runs." The high, thin voice dropped to almost a whisper. "He don't give a fuck who he hurts."

"You don't need to tell me."

"But you called him."

She tired of thinking of him as reedy, the ghost, the man who might rape her—he needed a name. This blindfold was making her crazy. The pain was making her crazy. "Water."

Silence.

"Please."

She heard his steps; their sound receded. He'd either walked away or stopped but he hadn't said anything. He had a reedy voice, she'd call him Lou. She had to give him a name, and she liked some Lou Reed songs. Her head hurt and she had heartburn she hadn't even thought about. It had been there since the pain. The pain mattered more. She needed to calm down, to slow down, she needed water and she needed sleep and she needed out of here more than anything. If she had to fuck this guy to get out that was nothing, she'd fucked guys she didn't like before. It had been a while, and she didn't want to go back to those years, but she'd survived them and she'd survive this dick. Unless he actually killed her. Jesus, he might. He might kill her.

Footsteps approached.

"Lou?"

"Sit up."

She was weak, it was hard to rise from where she lay. When she wasn't beat up she could do a hundred stomach crunches easy, but she struggled to sit up for him.

An unfamiliar hand braced her lower back, pushed her the rest of the way up. At least her T-shirt was between his hand and her back.

"Tip your head," he said.

"Why?"

"So you can drink."

"Untie me."

Maybe she said it enough like a command. He got behind her, untied her.

She held out her hands but her wrists were sore. Too far apart for a cup to go between them. "Put it in one hand," she said. "But leave your hand there long enough I can hold it with both."

He held the cup to her right hand. She brought her left hand over and pressed against his hand long enough to secure a two-handed grip on the cup. She pulled her legs under her ass and sat up straight. She drank.

"Who's Lou?" he asked.

Olivia finished her gulp, tried to look at him through her blindfold. "You are. You have to have a name."

"It ain't Lou. I hate Lou."

She took another sip. "Think how I feel. But I'm sure you're just doing your job. What's your fucking job,

Lou?"

"Gimme Dust," Lou said. "That's my job."

"Yeah, Lou? I bartend. Sometimes I got a bar full of assholes, drunk assholes. My job is to make them all tip good. And not let them think they can fuck me."

"You know someone named Lou?"

"I don't even know you."

"If you don't know no one named Lou, why call me that?"

"You remind me of Lou Reed."

"I fucking hate Lou Reed."

"Yeah," Olivia said, "he probably did too."

"Look." Lou put his hands on Olivia's shoulders, held tight. They were large hands. "You got a pretty face, even one side marked up."

Oh God, here we go.

"You don't want the other side marked up."

Weird line if this was rape. "What the fuck are you talkin' about?"

"Look," Lou said again. His voice had a wheeze to it. Like maybe he had a lung problem. Like he was old and sickly and he already had his hands on her and next he'd be inside her. Like he wanted to do it nice because he was an old man and he clung to that much decency. Enough to tell himself rape wasn't rape.

"Are you gonna fuck me?"

"Jesus," he said, and Olivia knew she was right. He was old and had some sort of gentleman's code, like it was okay to rape but wrong to talk about it. She almost cut a man like that once. Bastard walked away. Lou probably wouldn't.

"But that's the threat, right? If I can't give you Dust, you gotta fucking rape me as punishment. Well if that's the idea, you oughta take the blindfold off so I can see how goddamn ugly you are and truly suffer. Really, is your dick that bad? In the dark, whose dick is that bad?"

"Shut up." His voice was weak.

Olivia was glad to comply. Beat to hell as she was, that speech damn near killed her.

But she had to continue, she had the upper hand. "Lou."

"Don't call me that."

It was weird. He had all the fucking control, but he was a man so he didn't know it. "You talk like you want me. I work in a bar, a lot of men want me. But you want me to talk about Dust more than you want to fuck me."

He slapped her, hard. She screamed. He covered her mouth and she bit his hand. He recoiled, backhanded her harder than the initial slap. She fell back on the bed and cried, yelled, coughed. Noises hard to define, as though her whole body spoke incoherently at once.

"Shut up!" Lou had her shoulders and shook them. He was on the bed with her this time, his face on hers. He kissed her. His lips were dry but she already lay on her back, she couldn't pull back. She turned away. Realized her hands were free, pulled her blindfold up.

She pushed her hands backward into the mattress and sat up, looked at Lou on her legs. She saw his straw-thin hair, prematurely gray. He was fifty at most, with a red pockmarked face like a minefield exposed.

"Stop," she said.

He slid a gnarled hand up under her shirt, grabbed one tit. "Give me Dust."

"Fuck me then. Asshole."

The hand that didn't hold a tit slapped her and Olivia

threw a punch across Lou's chin. He pulled his head back and she sat up farther. He didn't look hurt, just pushed her down again, held her by the throat with one hand, brought the other down outside her jeans and rubbed around her crotch.

"So you go back to your bosses," Olivia said, "tell them you got this and no Dust, they good with that?"

Lou kept rubbing. "They know I got everything I could from you."

"Rape means you raped," Olivia said, "don't mean shit else. Killing me's no good too. Never get anything from me that way. Your problem is, you need to know what the fuck you're doing."

"You saying I don't?"

"I don't want you and you touched me like I do. Fuck you."

He throttled her neck with one hand and she couldn't even gasp—no air. His other hand yanked at her jeans, tried to pull them off. Nothing gave. His strangling hand dropped to join the other. Her head fell back as he unbuttoned the top button, then the next. She struggled to breathe.

He was at the third button when her breath came back. She looked around her, saw nothing to hit him over the head with. Only one more button after this then her pants were down and she was getting raped. She wasn't strong enough to fight him. If she saw how, she was sure she could kill him. This was going the other way if she didn't.

Lou opened the bottom button and yanked but Olivia sat up on her ass and the jeans went nowhere. "You wanna fuck me," she said, "show me your dick."

"That ain't what this is about."

Olivia smiled up one side of her mouth, the side of her face that hadn't been cut. "Like hell it ain't." She sat a little taller, propped up with one hand on the bed. With the other she gently pushed at Lou's chest. "You know I got nothin' on Dust. And plenty for you." Her free hand stroked the thigh of his pants. "I just wanna live."

"Stand up a second," Lou said. "Get these pants to drop."

Olivia swung her legs off one side of the bed. You've already lost, Lou. If you think fucking me means anything. She stood. The pants stuck just below her hips. "I might have to call you another name. Lou wouldn't care so much."

"What?"

"You know that Bowie song?" Olivia said. "'She turns me on but we're only dancing?'"

Lou waved a hand. "Move your legs."

"You don't know the song?" Olivia shrugged but the pants stayed where they were.

Lou reached out and tugged.

"We're only gonna be dancing, Lou. And you put on a condom or you gotta kill me some other way. I ain't goin' by some guy's dirty dick."

He slapped her and she hit the floor.

Olivia looked up. "You dumb enough to fuck a strange woman without one?"

Lou shook his head. "I ain't got. That ain't what this was gonna be about."

"And one of us catching the other's AIDS, is that worth you raping me?"

"I ain't got it!" Lou said. "You?"

"Ain't been tested in a while." Olivia got into a squat.

Maybe she could defend herself now. "How many whores since you tested?"

"Aaaah!" Lou kicked, but Olivia moved a little and he missed.

Dust or Rico would break you, this guy might break himself.

"You don't work for Rico, do you?"

"Me? No." Lou looked embarrassed.

"So, look. Rico damn near killed me, left knowin' I knew nothin'. Said give him a call soon as I know anything. How about I do that same deal with you, only I call you first. You gotta move fast when I call, though. I don't call Rico right after, he's killin' me. Cool?"

Olivia held out a hand to shake.

Lou bent down and swatted the hand away. He looked frazzled. "You can't go until I know."

"Where Dust is? I won't find out here."

"It ain't right!" Lou kicked again. This time the toe of his boot came up under Olivia's chin, knocked her on her back.

The girl was a lot of trouble. Girls always were. She was worth it if he found Dust. The bounty on that boy would fix a whole lot of problems. Not his health, he'd live with that pain 'til he died. But that bitch he married, man she ran a tab. Good thing he didn't gamble. Or drink much. He had one now but he needed it.

That gal on the rug stirred up the stress, gave him a headache all over. Mostly it hurt his throat. Didn't take much to hurt his throat. That bitch hurt it bad.

Cobb hated the way she tried to play him. Smart mouth never was a good thing on a woman. Not on a man either. Now that she knew he'd hit her, maybe she'd stop that mouthy shit and tell him what she knew. God knows he didn't want to fuck her. Not with that messed up face. She lay unconscious. Blood dripped slowly from her chin onto her neck.

She might have been pretty before, but Cobb didn't live in the past. He worked part time since the cancer. Didn't have the strength for long days anymore. He sat on the edge of the mattress and took another slug from the bottle, set it down on the bedside table.

This would be a good time to walk around the room, but even that little fight with the bitch wore him out. She'd be out a while longer, maybe by then he'd feel like standing. He should put the blindfold back on for when she did wake up, but that could wait a few minutes.

He figured she'd have a headache when she woke, hell, probably had one in her dreams. She deserved it. He didn't deserve the one she gave him. Ask a simple question, get a simple answer, game over. Not such a simple game now, not since she saw him. He wasn't going away again, he didn't have enough time left to spend any of it in prison. The bitch was dead when this was done.

"Get up." Lou's voice. "And don't bother screamin', ain't no one gonna hear. I mean, go ahead if you want."

Olivia sat on a couch, blindfold on again. She pushed herself up off the soft cushions. She hadn't noticed their softness while she sat. It wasn't enough to ease her pain, which was everywhere. She wobbled as she stood.

"You can stretch a while," Lou said. "I know you ain't stood lately."

"I'm exhausted," Olivia said. No attempt at deception there.

"Sit if you want. I'm going to." She heard furniture creak under his weight, somewhere in front of her. "It's a comfortable couch."

She sat.

"You want," he said, "to talk about Dust?"

"Yeah. But I don't know a fuckin' thing."

"I don't mean where he went," Lou said. "I mean when you were together."

"Oh."

It sounded like an invitation to talk about nothing. She figured she could do that. It was different than before, when she talked about nothing because it was all she knew.

"He was exciting because he was a criminal, even though he wouldn't say what he did. It wasn't like he worked in a bank. And he liked me a lot, that's always nice. But it was an affair, it was shit. I thought it might get better. He drank a lot. It got worse."

"He didn't say what he did?"

"He beat guys up sometimes, that much was obvious. How he got paid for that, I don't know."

"He acted like an enforcer?"

A brief grin crossed Olivia's lips. "There were hurt knuckle nights." The grin left her face. "Then I could help him. Ease the pain. That was nice."

"He didn't tell you how he hurt them?"

"I asked, he never said. I think he protected me too much." She said it blindfolded and expecting to die, and thought: Dust didn't protect me nearly enough.

***

Oakland was bloody. Nothing unusual there, but Berkeley was bloody too. The towns were side by side and there was violence in both, but Berkeley was a university town, the focus was on the achievements of the educated masses, not the occasional shootings in bad neighborhoods. In Oakland, every minute was a possible occasion. Right now, two gang bosses with a history of malevolent cooperation had a dispute that crossed city borders. This violence was shared.

When Keene referred to his Berkeley house, he didn't mean his home. His home was where he lived with his wife, a place no one went, in conversation or otherwise. Keene's house was a house of business, in a nice, residential neighborhood. The kind of business Keene did there couldn't be zoned for.

Keene didn't take much counsel during war. He had men he talked to, advice he heard, but overall strategy? He'd been in this for years, knew what he had, knew what he could lose. Who he could lose. There were always pawns to sacrifice.

Keene had a man in his Berkeley house he would normally meet in public. Not during this war—going outside was a risk. They sat at a round table Keene used for small meetings, nothing to artificially imply power for the host. He had bodyguards on the walls and throughout the house, of course. And he met with a man he trusted implicitly. Who had been thoroughly frisked in the front hall. Easier to trust a man implicitly if he was unarmed.

Willis, tall and thin with a businessman's short haircut, sat across the table from Keene. His short-sleeved plaid shirt wasn't tucked in.

Both men's hands rested palms down on the table.

Keene laced his fingers, cracked his knuckles. "2731 Hunter. Been mine for years, a safe house for runners. I'm expecting someone there, and I want you to handle it. Take Platt and Tré. The men there now know you're coming. They leave when you get there."

"Platt?" Willis said. "Who you expecting?"

"A man you can't lose."

"Platt—he's a fucking hitter."

Keene's palms returned to their place on the table. "I didn't say he can't die. I said you can't lose him."

Dust worked for Keene a lot of years ago. A good worker, but he had banks in mind. Keene didn't give a fuck about banks. Too much risk, not enough money. Keene took the easy prey: drugs, weapons, gambling, whores. Risk was for losers. The war with Lee might kill him; more likely they'd both survive, winning and losing determined by who walked away with the most. They'd do business again, only one would have the upper hand. Keene liked his odds, figured Lee liked his. They were both smart. One of them was wrong.

Dust was about to become the next distraction, if what Keene heard was true. It was a guess, but a good one. Dust was on the run. If he returned to the East Bay, he'd need shelter backed by muscle. If Dust came to him, it would have to be with a business proposition. Keene doubted that Dust had ripped off enough to offer anything that mattered.

Keene didn't need this shit. He had a war with Lee, which cut into profits and resources and kept him inside even more than usual. He had nothing against Dust, but helping him might make an enemy of Tenny. Tenny on his own didn't scare him, but if he threw in with Lee? Wasn't worth the risk. And if he did Tenny a favor, Tenny had soldiers.

He sent his bodyguards out of the room, sat alone at the table. A room without windows, without anything but soundproof walls, the table and chairs, and the desk on the wall behind him. And the contents of the desk, which included a fifth of Yamazaki, a Japanese single malt that was Keene's favorite. Glasses in the desk as well, and a cloth for wiping them. Keene poured himself a glass and drank as he thought about war, and how much Tenny would trade for Dust.

Platt filled the passenger seat comfortably, fit but wide, prison tats—snakes and crosses, daggers and chains—on his arms and neck. "Why we goin' to this place?" It wasn't the first time he'd asked.

Willis drove. "For Keene." Not the first time he'd answered. "A guy needs to be handled. Might not be easy. We're trusted."

Maybe Platt got it this time. Anyway, he shut up. The house they drove to was suburban. Whatever they did would have to be done quiet. That was where Willis figured to work hardest, stopping Platt from firing a gun. Where his focus had to be, why Keene's operation included a third man. Tré was a steady hand, if not as brutally efficient as Platt. Which was fine. One man like Platt would take care of all the brutality necessary.

Willis and Platt rode with windows down, the trunk filled with Platt's shit, stuff he might need on the job. Tools and cleaning supplies, like he was a fucking handyman.

Between Platt's place and the house on Hunter Street they drove past a Church's Chicken. The crowd on the sidewalk out front of Church's gave them a near contact high's worth of weed.

Platt had messy hair that hung just above his shoulders, tats visible everywhere except on his face, and big knuckles, like he'd punched a few walls. Or heads. He looked at the crowd then back at Willis. "Damn if I know how anyone lives like that. I mean, look at those people, you know they ain't homeless, they just outside. I can see if you fell so far you had no choice, got crazy and slept on sidewalks and that shit. But look at them. They out here every day and night, bummin'. Don't know how they can stand it. If I had nothin' I wouldn't ask for nothin'. Just take it. Fuckin' take it and fuck up anyone try to stop me."

Willis kept his eyes on the road. "You won't be out there cuz you got skills."

"Balls is what it is. Those pussies fight, over smokes or chicken legs or slugs from a bottle, they too weak to kill each other. Like anyone care if they did. That's your power out there, do what you want cuz no one give a fuck. About you, about none a them. Take from each other and ain't no one got nothin'."

Willis had heard Platt philosophize before. The man had thoughts, but mainly he had murder on his mind. "You just wanna be a street sweeper."

A moment where all they heard were the cars and their stereos and the people outside. Then Platt laughed. "Yeah, but this Keene shit…you know…it's like we're in a war and we always dodge it."

"Keene won't expose his best soldiers," Willis said. "We're that."

"We ain't soldiers if we don't fight."

Willis took a left at the light. "We ain't soldiers if we die."

"After we die," Platt said. "We ain't soldiers after we die. Soldiers fight to the death."

"Not to mine," Willis said. "I fight to someone else's."

Olivia sat blindfolded on the couch, only her hands free. She could smell Lou nearby.

"So," Lou said, "you liked Dust because he was dangerous. But he didn't tell you what he did."

It wasn't worth saying a word, but shaking her head would hurt. She hesitated. Was yes or no the answer that said he didn't tell her?

"Right," she said.

"Then how was he dangerous?"

"He..." Olivia's hands fumbled in the air. "With Rico. Those two guys sat at the bar, it wasn't like when other guys sat at the bar."

"He picked you up and you went somewhere."

"My place," Olivia said. "I didn't know he didn't have a place."

"You mean he shared it. How'd you feel about that?"

"What the fuck, you my therapist?"

"I got a gun aimed at your head."

Olivia's hands moved again. Her body was stuck on the couch. "I—I knew he was with someone. Guys like that are. I didn't want to keep him. Didn't know I'd like him."

"You liked him the first night?"

"Yeah."

"And you knew what about him then?"

"What I figured at the bar. He had an edge, but he was a nice guy."

"A nice guy?" Lou asked.

"He was always nice to me. Then."

"Before what?"

"Before he hit me with a glass."

"Something," Lou said, "changed between nice and that."

Olivia started to shrug, winced and her shoulders dropped. "You start with a guy, everything's low-key." Her shoulders tightened, like she considered shrugging again, thought better of it. "He moves in, work has him stressed but he won't talk, he just drinks. It was bad at the end and I told him. He got all defensive and hit me."

Lou was quiet a minute. "Okay. What was it like when things were good? What did you talk about?"

Her neck was strong enough now. Olivia shook her head. Her lips turned up. "Nothin'." No smile now. "We drank and we fucked."

"Then the fucking stopped and he hit you?"

Olivia glared. "Fuck you."

"Bad time to get sensitive."

"You think you scare me now?" Olivia stood. "You think I ain't been scared for days?"

"I want more," Lou said, "about when you liked him."

"I always liked him."

Lou gave her half a minute.

She kept her mouth shut.

"This ain't one a them silence is gold things, honey. Idea is, you talk 'til I hear something I can use. You stop when I say."

119

"It wasn't deep. It was sex. He wanted me and I wanted him."

"Had to be something else."

"Besides sex? Sometimes we'd listen to music, we'd talk. Only he never said much. I asked what he did, he'd say I couldn't know. One night I got home after work and he was there and it was bad. He said he hurt someone and now someone else wanted him dead. He said he thought they might kill him. The next night he—" Her hand covered her bruised, scarred cheek. Tears started again. "It's the most he ever said about his job."

"The night before he left." Lou stood, walked away.

Cobb drove, Olivia in back. The shot he gave her would keep her asleep for the drive. She was out so deep she didn't try to turn over when he lay her down on her wounded cheek.

Maybe Dust killed Davis, maybe not. Either way, he didn't leave town until he was accused. Sounded like he was stressed the night before. Like he was planning something one night and hell broke loose the next. If he'd ripped off a regular guy instead of Tenny, only the cops would care.

Dust used to work for Keene, and Keene was in Berkeley. Less than two hours away. If Dust went anywhere else, by now he was gone. Cobb drove with the fast traffic. He probably didn't need the girl anymore. He'd make sure of that before he killed her.

Carelli could usually be found at a place right off the freeway. There was a free public lot a block from there, for local shoppers. Rico parked, locked up, and walked.

An outdoor table at Starbucks was where Carelli liked to sit. Rico knew that much from a phone call. He had the man's home address in case he wasn't at the table, but the guy he talked to was pretty sure he would be. Rico didn't like being in another town, relying on a guy he'd never met just because the guy was supposed to know a lot. Like the way he was supposed to know it was Carelli—he wouldn't have a phone or a laptop, just a newspaper. Rico didn't even have a photo of the man, just a description. Carelli never got busted, didn't let his picture get taken.

Starbucks had several outdoor tables. At one of them sat a small skinny white guy with glasses, thinning hair, and an open newspaper.

Rico stepped to the man's table. "Carelli?"

The man finished his sip of coffee, looked up from his newspaper. "Word is you ain't stupid, Rico."

Already sounded like a man Rico should talk to. "You know why I'm here?"

"Siddown." Carelli pointed at the metal chair across from him. "You ain't usin' force, right?"

Rico sat. "I didn't drive this far to die."

Carelli gave a short laugh. "What's in it for me?"

"Money." Rico glanced at Carelli's nearly full cup. He hated these big coffee chains. Long lines and no damn table service.

"What brings you to Oakland, Rico?"

Rico looked around. No one sat close enough to hear. He spoke soft. "A guy who works for me might be down here. I need him back."

Rico held a little notebook, patted every pocket he had. "Got a pen?"

Carelli shook his head. A college age kid with a laptop sat at the table next to them.

"Hey, kid," Rico said to the boy, "got a pen I can borrow?"

"Yeah, sure." The kid was skinny with sloppy long hair. Rico hated him on sight, was glad to use him.

"Thanks." Rico took the pen the boy held out, wrote on one page from the notebook, tore out the page and handed it to Carelli, gave the pen back to the boy.

Carelli looked at the name, returned the slip of paper to Rico.

"You won't do it? Or you already know?"

"Now I know the name," Carelli said. "I won't walk around with it. You got a picture?"

Rico shook his head. "He don't advertise."

"Smart man," Carelli said. "He done time?"

The kid looked over at them. Rico looked back at the kid. "Go the fuck away." He said it in a voice no unarmed man would question.

The boy closed his laptop, moved to the farthest open table.

Rico looked at Carelli. "Yeah. Hard."

"You want him how bad?"

Rico looked around again, looked back at Carelli. "Five large. And I need him now."

"All of it up front," Carelli said. "I stop when I find him. No refunds, no excuses. My time is valuable, this won't take long. And the price is ten."

"Let's walk."

Carelli nodded, folded his newspaper, set his cup on top and stood.

"I brought five," Rico said. They walked. "Five more, I need results."

"You pay five for no results? I take it."

"You know what I fucking mean." Rico didn't like this guy. Needed him though. "I go into a bank, get five more, it's all yours. But I get results."

"Ten large and I find him. A man's word is his life."

On the street, yeah. Or you use muscle and cross the fucker you promised.

"I'm with Tenny," Rico said.

"Nice insurance," Carelli said. "Don't fucking matter. A man's word is his life. I already promised."

A lotta guys promise, Rico thought, but you don't say shit like that to a man like Carelli. Rico had a bank nearby and they walked there.

Carelli waited near the bus stop outside the bank.

After a few minutes Rico came out, handed over an envelope. "Like you wanted, forty-nine sixty in bills." His other hand came out of a pants pocket. "And forty in quarters. What the hell?"

"I use pay phones."

Rico laughed. "Where the fuck you find pay phones?"

"Bus station. Where you parked?"

They walked and Rico wondered. Little dude was weird, paranoid as hell, but he was in with everyone and the cops never touched him. Maybe weird was good.

Rico's car was a short walk. They got in. "How long you use pay phones?"

"I'm not a young man."

Okay, fuck paranoid, this guy didn't say shit. "I done this a long time. Never met a guy like you."

Carelli nodded. "Take a right to get out of the lot. Another at the corner, then one lane over. Through the first light and a left at the next."

Rico hated Carelli at first. Now he joined him in the silence, drove.

Downtown Oakland Greyhound had pay phones and cable TV. Basketball was on a big screen. Rico stood behind people sitting and watching, some of them probably homeless but how do you tell that from the usual Greyhound customers? Except the obvious winos with their blankets. They just sat there, weren't loud right now. Maybe they'd get chased if they weren't quiet. Maybe. Oakland had bigger problems.

Rico stood sideways so he could watch Carelli on the phones, but when he looked Carelli mostly wasn't talking. No way to tell if anything was being said on the other end. Every couple minutes if he timed it right he saw Carelli drop quarters in. Word was the man knew everyone and everything in Oakland.

Must have been an hour when Rico walked over. He got fifteen feet from the phone, waited. Carelli saw him. Rico tipped his head back. Carelli finished his call and joined him.

"This ain't your usual calls," Rico said.

Carelli shook his head. "Your man's a stranger."

"So he's easy to see."

"Would be if he was here."

"If?"

"You forget," Carelli said. "I keep the money only when you get him. You'll get him."

Rico nodded but he wasn't sure. Tenny needed more than any man's word.

One side of Carelli's mouth grinned. It didn't look happy. "Go watch hoops." He turned around, returned to his phone.

Rico walked back, wished he knew the spread on to-day's games, wished he gave a fuck.

Carelli stepped away from the phone. He'd been on it a long time, one call after another.

Rico had an eye on him the whole time, met him halfway. "You get somethin'?"

"Gimme some coffee. I gotta make follow-up calls."

"Follow-up?" First hint of hope Rico heard yet.

"Someone maybe saw him. Gotta get details."

Carelli glared. Rico looked around, saw a coffee machine, walked to it, watched Carelli. Carelli wouldn't cut out but trust didn't go farther than point blank range. If someone came to Carelli, Rico would see.

Carelli had quarters in the phone before Rico had dollars in the overpriced coffee machine—no way this shit tasted like real coffee but they sure as hell charged like it. Rico got one for himself too, with the artificial cream and sugar, and sipped. Worse than prison Folgers, but he wasn't doing years at Greyhound.

He walked to the phone and handed Carelli his coffee. Carelli took it without looking, intent on the phone, nodding. He took a long drink of the hot muck, hung up. "We should go."

Carelli didn't smile, but he said it like it was good news. Rico hadn't had good news since before Dust ripped off Tenny.

An alley in East Oakland, trash cans knocked over between brick walls, shit too big to be a dog's on the pocked asphalt, although maybe not going by the size of the scampering rats. Rico didn't know Oakland but he knew alleys like this. "We get what we want fast or we leave."

"He meets us here." Carelli spoke soft. "Or he don't meet us."

"I get bit by a goddamn rat," Rico said, "he talks then he dies."

"He don't go where he might get followed."

Rico shook his head at the muck he stood in. Probably not shit, just whatever spilled and leaked here. Probably. "I can tell."

It was afternoon but between buildings it was almost dark. They stood there like they were calm. No one with sense could be. Men don't wait for men in Oakland alleys unarmed. Rico sure didn't.

Less than an hour and a man entered the alley. Middle-aged, dark hair, blue jeans with a matching vest and a white T-shirt. Eyes wide, high on something. Good, Rico thought, a man with a cause.

Barely in the alley and Carelli spoke. "Where is he? Then I help you out."

"Two hours," the man said. His skin was dark, maybe just a tan but there was a trace of an accent. Mexican? He aimed a thumb backward. "Telegraph. Near Grand. He got a burger."

"You know it's him how?" Carelli asked.

"Oh, I know Dust. Rumors 'bout him inside. I stay clear."

"Then or now?" Carelli said.

"And. Twice I don't die."

Rico nodded. Didn't recognize this guy, but Dust earned some rep inside. Protection you get from who you hang with. Rep you get on your own.

"Which way'd he go?" Carelli asked.

"My money?"

"Which way first."

"Got in his car eating, headed downtown."

Carelli looked at Rico. "Twenty."

Rico got the bill from his wallet, held it out and the guy grabbed it. Rico held on. "You lied, you dead."

Wide-eyes shook his head fast, tried to back up with the bill. Rico let go and the speedfreak stumbled, crumpled the bill in his hand as he turned and ran.

"All this shit on our shoes," Rico said as they walked out of the alley, "we get outta my car, I'm gonna need it Martinized."

Rico drove straight, turned where Carelli said. "You know where he'd go downtown?"

"He's not lookin' for work, is he?" Carelli rolled his window down.

"Just holin' up, I'd guess." Rico's window went down too.

"He could buy good protection down this way, but he's gonna stand out in Chinatown. The guy I'd expect is the other direction."

"Any good sections for a white man in Oakland?"

"Yeah," Carelli said. "My house." He laughed.

"So where's he go?"

"The freeway's just past downtown. He could go anywhere. If he stays local, Berkeley's full of white men."

"Shit," Rico said. "We gotta send guys that way."

"Made that call before we left Greyhound. Another hunch to play while we're down here. There's a bar up a couple blocks, I got a source there. Park when you can."

Next block Rico saw a space on the opposite side of the street. He swung a tight U-turn and paralleled in.

"Big car moves nice," Carelli said.

"Lincoln fucking Continental."

Traffic cleared and they walked across the middle of the street. Bar was on the next block, banner over the door: The Big House. Great, Rico thought.

Early in the day the place wasn't crowded, wasn't empty either. Mostly black customers, old men not looking down on their luck, just drinking in the afternoon.

The bartender walked over, a fiftyish black man in a flowery shirt, his cheeks full and nose flattened, like he'd had plenty of times of his own, not all of them good. He nodded at Carelli. "Coffee?"

"You got it, Jermain. My friend's buying." He turned to Rico. "I'll be right back."

Carelli walked across the room to the men's room door. Rico watched him go in and took a seat at the bar, glanced at the beer selection. "Anchor for me." It wasn't a light beer, but Rico could down it as fast as Carelli's questions were answered. He wished he knew what they were so he could start this himself. He opened his wallet, set a ten on the bar, took a drink from his beer as soon as it was in front of him. Jermain set a black coffee at the place to Rico's left and picked up the ten.

Jermain set the change down.

"This your place?" Rico asked.

"My wife left me forty years ago. Started drinking myself to death, saw all the money I was throwing away. Thought I'd get in on it."

Jermain turned away and Carelli came back. Rico let his change sit.

Carelli took a sip of coffee. "Jermain."

The bartender came back, looked at Carelli, kept his mouth shut.

"A man named Dust, worked local a ways back, banks and side jobs, remember?"

"Good guy," Jermain said, "mean drunk. Liked to drink."

Carelli looked at Rico.

Rico nodded. "That's him. And a lotta other guys."

Jermain ran a finger across his nose. "He liked the ladies too. And he liked to leave 'em. He'd come down here, act like he was the one hurt by it. Had ladies convinced they could cheer him up when he was down. But he was always down."

"Go on," Rico said. "Where is he?"

"If he's here now he's gone to Mimi Lee. Chinatown somewhere. I can get the address."

"Do that," Carelli said.

"It's in back, you get it in a minute, but first thing Mimi's gonna do is tell him get out. Then he goes to Berkeley."

Carelli looked in his coffee, then back at Jermain. "Keene?"

Jermain nodded.

"Get Mimi's address."

Jermain looked around the bar. No one needed a refill. He stepped through a swinging door behind the bar.

Rico stood, set his empty glass on the table just as Jermain came back and handed Carelli a small slip of paper.

Carelli glanced at it, raised his eyebrows, stood with Rico. "I know that building. Five minutes from here. Mimi won't let us in but Keene's a half hour away and him we don't see without an appointment."

* * *

Rico drove to Mimi's. Five minutes to drive maybe, but Chinatown was a hard place to park. Ten minutes to park four blocks away, five minutes to walk four crowded blocks, bustling as fast as possible through the young, the old, the confused.

Carelli stopped outside a narrow doorway. Two steps up to the apartment house callbox. Rico stood there, stared at it. All the writing was in Chinese. He looked back at Carelli. "How we get in?"

Carelli grinned. "How's your Mandarin?"

Rico glared but Carelli ignored him, stepped up to the box, pressed a button.

A woman spoke through the box, must have been Chinese. Carelli answered, sounded like the same language. A buzzer sounded and Carelli pushed the front door open.

Rico was right behind him. "You said Mimi wouldn't let us in."

"That wasn't Mimi."

Rico's phone buzzed in his pocket. He grabbed it tight, looked at the number. Vollmer. He answered. "You in Oakland?"

"Berkeley. She just went into a house."

"Fuck. He there?"

"Someone let her in," Vollmer said. "Couldn't see who."

"Stay with her. I'll call back."

Carelli started up a narrow staircase. Rico came up behind him, too wide to fit alongside. There was a musty smell in here. Nothing was dirty but the carpet looked a million years old, the paint job about the same. And somewhere up the stairs was another broad Dust liked. Another one with the sense to kick him out.

Carelli and Rico went up the stairs fast and quiet, reached the second floor landing and Carelli turned down the hall. Rico followed. Carelli stopped at a door and banged on it. Rico fell back against the wall. One hand went to the pistol in his coat.

Chinese words in a woman's voice came from the other side of the door.

Carelli spoke Chinese back.

The door opened a crack.

Carelli kicked it wide open. He stepped into the room and Rico followed. A small, beautiful Chinese woman stood there, too close for her own good. Carelli swung a mean right into her gut and the woman fell back. She hit the carpet and Rico shut the door.

Carelli stepped forward, his legs wide enough apart to straddle Mimi's lean body. He looked down. "Dust. Where?"

Mimi was about thirty, angled jawline, too much mascara emphasized her wide eyes. "He's here five minutes. Gone."

"What did he want?"

"To stay."

Carelli kicked her in the cheek and her hands came up as she rolled on her side. "Where'd he go?"

"No," she said.

Carelli dropped, rolled her by the shoulders and lay her on her back as his knee came down soft on her neck. "Where?"

"I don't know."

Carelli looked back at Rico, stood and stepped away as Rico moved forward.

Rico kneeled, his knee beside Mimi's head. He spoke, his voice barely above a whisper. "Sit up."

Mimi lay there. Rico helped her until she sat with legs crossed.

He squatted in front of her. "You okay?" Mimi was young. If Dust hadn't seen her in years, how old was she then?

"No."

Rico looked at Carelli. "Well, he's a dick. But he's not as bad as Dust."

Mimi sat across from him, her dark brown eyes a flame that wouldn't change, the brows above them painted thin, arched. She said nothing.

Rico didn't expect her to talk. He stood slowly, the index finger of one cupped hand under her chin. She stood with him. Rico was a foot taller and at least twice her weight. He kept his index finger under her chin, tilted her lean jaw up at him.

"Dust knew you how long ago?"

"Seven years." An accent to her voice, no hesitation in her answer. The answer too precise, like she'd kept track of the time.

"What did he want today?"

"A place to stay."

"Bullshit. What did he want?"

Mimi's blank face dropped. She looked beautiful sad. "I tell him Keene. Always got work."

Rico slapped her hard across the face and Mimi fell, crying. Rico dropped down, his face just over hers. He yelled: "Who else does he go to? Who?!"

Mimi cried. "Just Keene. Just…"

Rico's hand went inside his coat, came out with brass knucks on. He brushed them against Mimi's cheek.

"Where's Keene?"

Mimi blinked fast, kept blinking, kept crying. "B—b—"

Rico's mouth dropped in front of hers. "Berkeley?"

Mimi lay on her back, nodded frantically, bumped her forehead against Rico's. He pulled back as she cried and gurgled.

Rico stood, grabbed his phone, called Vollmer. "What street are you on?"

Rico pulled up next to where Vollmer sat parked in his car, rolled down Carelli's passenger side window.

Vollmer's elbow jutted out of the car, a cigarette in his hand.

"Who else is in there?" Rico said.

"Couldn't see. They hardly opened the door, just let her in."

"And the boy?"

Vollmer smoked. "Yeah, he's with her."

Rico looked at Carelli. "This a Keene house?"

Carelli shrugged. "If it is, only way you get in is dead."

"Wait for them to come out," Rico said to Vollmer. "Or until I call."

Carelli shook his head. "You can't sit out front of a Berkeley house forever."

"There's guys comin' soon," Rico said. "Stone, a couple more besides. We rotate the watch."

"If cops come before then?" Vollmer asked.

"Go, then call me. If they ask why you're here, you're lost and you're tired."

"Lookin' for what?"

Rico looked at Carelli.

"India Palace," Carelli said. "A restaurant, lotta people know it."

Vollmer dropped his cigarette in the street, lit another. Rico and Carelli drove away.

Theresa sat on the living room couch, her arm tight around Jeremy. Three men in jeans stood close together just inside the doorway toward the back of the house. They stepped toward the couch.

The tall, thin man in front had a businessman's short haircut and wore a short-sleeved plaid shirt, untucked. He was flanked on one side by a black guy almost as tall, thick arms obvious in his white T-shirt, a long scar on his cheek and a holstered pistol on his hip. Other side of the tall man was the shortest of the three, a wider man with messy hair that stopped just above his shoulders, what looked like prison tats, and a bulky leather jacket that, by the way it hung, carried more than one weapon.

Theresa did her best not to show fear, figured things were going to get worse.

The tall man spoke. "Who you here for?"

"I'm looking for a man called Keene."

"Keene sees who he wants."

She waited for him to say more but he seemed to be done. "You're good as Keene to me," she said, "if you know where Dust is."

"Dust?" The tall man looked surprised. "Ain't heard that name in years."

"You know him?" Theresa asked.

"Knew," the tall man said. The men behind him damn

near looked asleep. "Dust left town years ago. Went south, I think."

"He might be back," Theresa said. "I gotta know."

"He break your heart?" The tall man smiled. "Or that bastard rip you off?"

"None of your business."

The tall man stood over her, put his hands on her shoulders and squeezed. "If it's business in this town, it's ours."

Theresa clenched her teeth so she wouldn't stammer, unclenched them and talked slow. "It's not like that."

The tall man let go of her shoulders. His thumb brushed along her cheek and he flashed a grin that under different circumstances might have passed for charming. "What's it like, honey?"

She cringed and he smiled wider. She shook her head and his hand dropped from her face.

"You might think I'll hurt you." He grinned again, a sadistic glint in his eyes. "I don't hurt people. People talk to me." He aimed a thumb at the burly, coated man behind him. "He hurts people. And he don't listen good. He got good pliers."

"Pliers?"

The tall man nodded.

Theresa tried to look calm, hoped Jeremy didn't feel the sweat from her palm. "Dust didn't take money from me. I got a visit. A man I didn't know."

"Men hurt you? Men scare you?"

"One man."

The tall man leaned in. "A stranger."

She nodded.

"Who'd Dust rip off?"

"He never talked about work."

"But you found your way here."

"He wrote down the address. He wrote Keene's name."

The tall man took a step back, spoke under his breath like it didn't matter. "Dust got any friends?"

"No," Theresa said. "Well, Rico. They used to meet in the morning."

The tall man nodded. "What do you know about Rico?"

"Dust had coffee with him, drinks with him. I think they worked together."

"Worked doing what?"

"I don't know," she said.

"Big dude?"

"I never saw him. But there were times Dust said he had to. Said it like he was in trouble if he didn't."

The tall man turned around, put an arm on the coated man's shoulder. As they walked out of the room he glanced at the black guy with the scar. "Watch them."

"Shut that," Willis said, and Platt shut the kitchen door behind them. Willis turned, faced Platt. "Ever see Rico? He's down south, came up here a couple times."

Platt shook his head. "Don't remember."

Willis smiled open mouthed, his teeth gleaming. "You'd remember if you saw him. Works for Tenny. Nasty."

"Nasty like gross?"

"Nasty like he better be on our side."

Platt shrugged. "Don't scare me."

Willis wasn't smiling anymore. "Don't be stupid. If he's against us, shoot him in the back."

ACT 4

Carelli leaned back as Rico drove. "Where we goin' now?"

"Where's Keene?"

Carelli shook his head.

"If he ain't a fool, he wants to talk to me. And unless you're a fool," Rico pulled a .45 from under his coat, stuck it in Carelli's ribs, "you take me to him."

"Take a right at the corner, then straight a while. When you turn again, it's a left. I'll tell you when we're close. And remember, you shoot me, a whole lotta guys comin' after you."

Rico nodded, got to the corner, turned. "When we met," he said, "how'd you know who I was?"

"I guessed."

Rico narrowed his eyes at Carelli. "Guessed."

"I knew about Tenny's money, knew your name. You're the guy he uses for jobs like that."

"So no one talked about me. But someone talked about Dust and the money."

"I'm a reporter, Rico." Carelli grinned. "I don't give up my sources."

Rico took his left hand off the wheel, cracked its knuckles against his chest. "But you sell information."

"I only sell it if it won't come back at me."

Rico wasn't patient. He asked questions to fill time until they got to Keene. He'd rather fill it with coffee and sandwiches. He'd rather go inside that house where he left Vollmer, see what was going on. "What you think goes on in there?"

"Keene's house?" Carelli asked. "Or the one we just left?"

"About to find out what happens at Keene's," Rico said. "The other."

"They got at least the broad. No one gets in uninvited."

"We know the broad's there," Rico said. "Vollmer said so. You tellin' me there's made men inside?"

"It's a safe house," Carelli said. "Not sure how safe during this war. But it's Keene's."

"So Keene has the girl. Maybe he got Dust too. And I can get in to see him."

"Keene?" Carelli shook his head. "I didn't say that, you did. You say it like we show up and he sees me." Carelli looked at Rico, but Rico was focused on driving. "I never been his place without an invite."

"Invite this, invite that. Berkeley's too fuckin' polite. That why Keene's losin' this war?"

Carelli shook his head. "Keene's been doin' this a while. What he loses don't mean as much as what he's gonna win."

"He's gonna win?" Rico glanced at Carelli.

"Territory he loses is hard to protect, not worth the effort. What he gains is close to his strongholds, gives him a stronger base."

"Keene's winning? Against Lee?"

"Lee's gonna hit hard soon," Carelli said, "try to stop it. Keene's waiting. You picked a bloody time to come here."

Rico stopped at a red light. "Everywhere I go's a bloody time."

Theresa and Jeremy remained huddled on the couch. She dreaded what might happen next but had to know. Maybe it wouldn't be the worst thing that could happen. Or maybe she didn't know what that was.

The black man with the scar and the pistol showed no emotion, no interest, just stood guard.

Theresa looked up at him. "What's your name?"

"Dumb question."

Theresa knew it was. But Jeremy had barely talked since they'd been taken at gunpoint, and she worried about him and worried about getting out of here. And wanted human interaction. Men did this treat the opposition like they aren't human bullshit all the time. Like caring about people was weakness.

"I'm Theresa. This is my son, Jeremy. He might not be scared, but he sure as hell has reason to be. Sorry I asked your name."

No answer.

"Is it Dust you wanna know about?" she said. "I don't know much. If it's Keene, I know nothin', it's just a name and address Dust wrote down. And he told me he used to work for him. Didn't say doin' what, and I don't care. I know Dust broke the law"—Jeremy's eyes went wide—"but I don't know what he did. I don't care what he did. I know he didn't kill a man, no matter what they said."

"Who said?"

"TV."

He shook his head, looked at her like she was an idiot. "TV don't know shit."

Here, this was casual conversation. The man who spoke knew how his part of the world worked. Dust could have killed Davis, but maybe he didn't.

"If Dust ripped off someone who wanted him caught, could the guy he robbed set him up for that? Murder, I mean."

Jeremy sat taller fast, stuck his face in front of hers. "Dust robbed someone?"

Theresa pulled her head back, put a hand on Jeremy's shoulder until his head returned to where it had been.

The scarred man's grin was gone. He glared at Jeremy, then Theresa. "If the man got power, his word is the word." His eyes squinted, face leaned toward her. "Now your guy's runnin' up here for protection?" He shook his head. "Wrong man to run to."

Theresa didn't answer.

"That name you mentioned at the end, he got my men back there strategizin'. Who's he?"

"Rico?"

The man nodded.

"I don't know. A guy Dust hung out with. Probably worked with. After Dust left, a guy showed up, knocked me around and threatened Jeremy. We left."

"And that was Rico?"

"Seemed too young," she said. "Maybe someone who worked for him."

"So you think Dust worked for Rico."

"Dust seemed like a man who'd never get scared. But sometimes when he said Rico's name..." Her voice trailed off. "I don't know who else."

"Could be anyone," the man said. "With the right

enemies..."

"Enemies," she said. A world with enemies was alien to her. People you didn't like, even hated, sure. But enemies, threats, people who might kill you. That was the world Dust had brought her into. Her and Jeremy. She couldn't forgive Dust for that. It was why she kicked him out. Should have done it sooner.

The tall man and his ugly companion returned to the room, pulled the scarred man aside. They walked away from Theresa and Jeremy, talked soft among themselves.

"Mom?" Jeremy said. "Why are we here?"

"I don't know what they want," Theresa said. "I'm going to find out."

"But you're the one who brought us here. I thought this was where he lived. The man Uncle Dust worked for."

"I don't know why he isn't here now. I only know he can help us."

"Where's Uncle Dust? When will he help us?"

From the mouths of babes. She shook her head. "Be patient, honey. When I find the man who knows him..."

"They sure don't treat us like guests. Uncle Dust wouldn't put up with this."

"I kicked him out, remember?"

"But you said the TV was wrong. And that guy," Jeremy pointed at the scarred man's turned back, "he agreed with you. I think."

"He said we can't trust TV. We should know that. We know Dust better than that."

"I hope so," Jeremy said.

They don't stay babes forever. She hugged her boy,

held him tight, didn't let him see that he was holding her up.

The ugly man walked slowly toward the couch, glared at them as he passed. Stopped at the window, looked outside a minute, returned to the tall man and whispered to him.

The tall man took in both other men in a glance, pointed a thumb toward the back of the house. "Wait in the kitchen. Both of you."

The tall man approached the couch as the other men exited the room. "Hey." He stood over Theresa and Jeremy, his narrow face over them like a bird ready to snatch worms.

"What?" she said, more a defensive pause than a word.

"You been followed. What the fuck's that about?"

"Followed?" she said. "Who? Why?"

"Tell me who, I figure out why. Who's your protection, bitch?"

"Do I look like I have protection?"

He took a step toward the couch. His right arm swung back then roundhoused open-handed at Theresa's cheek. She saw it coming and pushed Jeremy away. The palm caught her good and she flopped back across the couch. Her mouth popped open and a noise came out.

"Mom!" Jeremy crawled back to her end of the couch.

The tall man bent toward her but didn't grab her, like he knew how crazy a mom-protecting kid could get. "Who followed you?"

"Not my idea," she blubbered, just clear enough to be understood, crying. "I don't want to be followed."

The tall man stepped back. "Just lookin' for charity

and you think Keene's a donor."

"I don't know Keene." She bent forward and her long hair masked her face. Tears flowed. "Just tryin' to protect Jeremy. This is my whole family, here on this couch."

"Who followed you?" the tall man said.

"I don't know."

"Who?"

"I don't wanna be followed!"

"Yeah, well," the tall man said, "I go to a strange town, it's nice to have backup. You got backup, Theresa?"

"You know me? I don't know you."

"You don't wanna, believe me. So, you do have backup."

"No." Her voice was almost calm. "We snuck out. We coulda been followed, I don't know, I didn't see anyone. Never been followed."

"Maybe you never dealt with anyone who mattered. So, here's your minute in the big time. Only the big time ain't friendly. You want it over fast?"

Theresa shuddered, for herself and for Jeremy. Her lips slid back and forth while she figured how to say what had to be said. With her boy beside her. "Is that— that a threat?"

The tall man shook his head. "A question. Same question. Who coulda followed you? Think."

Theresa usually thought clearly. Right now her thoughts were all about surviving, getting herself and Jeremy out of this. She knew the other two men had guns, didn't see one on this guy.

The tall man grabbed a clump of her hair and pulled up hard. "Don't do me no good you don't tell me what you think."

"The man Rico sent." Theresa's eyebrows arched high, her eyes open wide. "I don't know his name."

"Describe him."

The tall man yanked her hair up higher.

Theresa sat up high and straight. "Shorter than you," she said, "but not short. Younger. Real young. And fit. In a leather jacket, but I could see he was strong. Felt it too." She ran an open palm slow across her cheek. "And he threatened us with a gun."

"You see it?"

"The gun?" Theresa didn't wait for an answer. "I don't know shit about guns, but it was big."

"He pulled it? Didn't just say he had one?"

"That thing was huge."

"Pistol?"

"Yeah," she said.

"See, you do know about guns."

"Even less than I know about sports. I watch movies is all."

The tall man grabbed her hair again. "Anyone else it coulda been?"

"Only Rico or guys who work with him. Guys like me, but not like this. Not psychos."

"Stable guys?" The tall man slid his hand down the back of her head, rested it softly against the bottom of her neck.

Theresa shook her head hard but the hand stayed. "Never heard of those."

Vollmer waited in the fucking car. He hated waiting, but he didn't know what might be inside the house. If Dust was there, the girl should be dead by now. Her only uses were for information and as bait.

His phone rang. Stone. He kept his eyes on the house, picked up. "Hey," he said. "I'm in Berkeley. Check this address." The numbers on the house he watched were hard to see. He read from the mailbox he was parked in front of. "Across the street from that, pretty sure it's a Keene house. Lemme know what you find out."

"I'll make some calls," Stone said.

Vollmer hung up. Warning was out, and Stone was sending backup. Vollmer turned off his phone.

He watched the nice goddamn house in the nice goddamn neighborhood, couldn't feel much more out of place. If he was casing the joint he had to get closer, look inside. He'd heard enough about Keene to assume the man was dangerous but he could check the place anyway, see if the girl was alive. If she was, the men inside were waiting for Dust and any motherfucker could watch this joint. Once he knew he'd call Rico, see if there was action somewhere else. Somewhere he could go and do something. Vollmer rolled up the windows, got out of the car, dropped his cigarette in the street, and crossed it casual as he could in a leather jacket no one would wear on a day this warm. It covered two pistols, and he wouldn't look near as casual if those were exposed.

There was no gate to get through, only a few steps up to a small porch. Ear and shoulder to the front door, he tried the knob slow—locked. He wasn't going in yet anyway, just checking. There were voices inside.

Fuck it. The door wasn't the way to go. The front window was small and tinted, no way to see in. He edged along the wall, his back to it. He'd see anyone coming out the front door. He looked suspicious as hell though, better get around the side where no one could see.

Around the corner—a gate with wood slats, pointed at the top. Seven feet high and locked. He looked back at the street. No one watched, and no windows from the house looked down on him. He could definitely vault that, try his luck around back. Vollmer reached, got a grip on the top of the gate and yanked. He was clearing the arrows when the wood caught him hard under the ribs, cracked the wood. He went through the top of the gate and plummeted, rolled when he hit ground, pushed himself up from the dirt and dropped straight back down. His ribs hurt like hell but he was in the back yard.

Crawled to the side wall and rested his back against it. Whatever was gonna happen better happen fast. But only after he got back up, and he wouldn't do that yet. Had to be full strength for this. He'd be on his feet again as soon as he could. If he stopped moving long he might need something for the pain. Wasn't as bad as a knife wound, though. He could fight his way through this, as soon as breathing didn't hurt anymore.

Breath accelerated on its own but the pain hit and he slowed it down, sat there wishing he could stop it completely. Not that he wanted to die, he just had to get back near full speed. He held his breath like that might help but he coughed, covered his mouth so he wouldn't be heard, went back to breathing slow, sat however many minutes it took until finally he thought he could stand without too much pain.

Vollmer couldn't reach the windows along the side of the house. He moved toward the rear, his back almost touching the wall, his hands on it like they propelled him as he stepped to his left. He dropped to a squat and peered around the corner. Nothing but shaded low-cut grass under a wooden back deck.

No wonder the windows along the side had been so high. The rooms inside weren't ground level, stairs led to the front door and to the deck in the back. Fuck. It was gonna be more of the same on the other side. If he was gonna see in, he had to make it up onto the back deck. And he'd be in clear view if anyone looked while he went up. But if he went back to the car and had to start over, he didn't know if he could clear that gate a second time. He should go back. His ribs were killing him from the first time, and that was a success.

But there was a woman inside, and women always made him think of Yula. Fuck, he wished they didn't. That wasn't his fault, she was a threat and that's what happens.

Vollmer stayed low, edged his way along the side of the deck. He stopped and turned his head. There were a couple of windows on that wall, he could at least look in.

He crept up the back porch steps, army crawled when he got to the top. Angled to the window farthest left, raised himself, and peered in. Seeing no one, just a round table with chairs in a small room, he squatted, crawled to his right, stopped at the next window and raised himself slow. He could feel it in his ribs. God-damn pain getting in his way.

A different room, a kitchen. Two men stood there, a tall black one and a thick white one. Neither man was Dust. They talked, but he couldn't hear. He had to see more than these two, needed a reason to go in or not. If he could get in the house without anyone knowing...

Maybe there was another way, around the other side of the house. But it looked like just front and back entrances. So long as these guys returned to the front of the house, didn't come out back, he'd see the door they went through, and it might be safe to break into the kitchen and listen through the door.

He waited and watched. He'd been quiet, no reason for them to look this way. They better not. If they saw him he'd have to kill them and Rico wouldn't like that. Might not mind if there was a good reason but Vollmer didn't have any fucking reason. Just a woman with her kid inside and the guys who took her. They only wanted her to talk about Dust. He hit her himself for the same damn reason but no way to know if these guys knew what they were doing. Anyway, he was the one who tailed her here. He didn't do that work to lose her to some assholes.

Tré's phone rang. Willis. Calling from the living room? He picked up. "Yeah?"

"Get in here," Willis said. "Both of you."

Tré opened the door and walked out of the kitchen. Platt followed, shut the door behind him. They went down the hall, entered the living room and stood with Willis. The other end of the room, Theresa held Jeremy tight on the couch.

"Our girlfriend here," Willis said, loud enough for Theresa and Jeremy to hear, "knows something after all. Before she hit the road to join us, she got knocked around a little. Guy worked for Rico, almost sure. So, the car outside?"

"Rico's boy?" Tré asked.

"Car outside?" Theresa's voice was soft. Only Jeremy looked at her.

"Whoever hit the bitch," Willis said, "that's who followed."

"Who's Rico?" Tré said. "What's he mean?"

"Works for Tenny," Willis said. "Big man down there. He's here, might be a lotta money in it. Worth talkin' to Theresa awhile."

"I'll talk," Platt's voice was almost a growl, like a meal was in front of him.

Willis smiled at Platt, pointed a thumb at Tré, his voice still loud. "He's better at talkin'. We use you if we need other techniques."

Both men out of the kitchen, Vollmer got up and ran off the porch. He could get through that back door any time, wouldn't follow two armed men who might turn around. He ran to the other side of the house. He leapt toward a high window, caught the outside windowsill easy, pulled himself up. His thick arms bulged and his belly strained as it stretched, his ribs like a knife sliced through them. He lifted himself high enough to lean his knees against the sill. Now the hard part.

He reached out with his left hand and tried the window, then pushed up as hard as he could with his right hand so he didn't fall. His teeth gritted as he probed with his left hand, got fingers under the bottom of the window and pushed it up enough to put his hand underneath. Breathing hard, he grinned as his left hand pushed up. The window squeaked.

If he fell going in it would make a helluva noise. The

window up as high as it went, Vollmer scraped his chest and belly as he crawled across the sill, his torso raw. He touched the floor with both hands, pulled his body tight and pushed it forward hard, somersaulted into the room and landed on the balls of his feet in a squat, barely made a sound.

Fuck, he didn't know he could do that. He got up slow and in pain. He wobbled as he stood, steadied himself in a minute. He walked forward too soft to be heard, looked side to side quickly. A spare bedroom, not cleaned any time recently.

He made his way to the closed door, leaned an ear against it and listened. Gave it a couple minutes, didn't hear a goddamn thing. Moved to the other side of the door and opened it a crack, peeked out.

There was a hallway and where it broke off to the left he could see a couch. Theresa and her boy were on it. It was all he could see. No voices but someone else had to be in the room or why stay on the couch?

Theresa whispered to Jeremy.

"Hey," a man's voice said. "No secrets here. Speak up."

Vollmer couldn't see the speaker but he had to be close to the couch or he would have talked louder.

Theresa turned to face the man. "Okay."

"Say it again. For me."

"I said don't worry," she said. "He's a little boy, what do you think I could say?"

"You coulda said anything. Every guy I work with used to be a little boy."

"Jeremy's not gonna be like the guys you work with." Theresa looked almost in tears.

"None of us was gonna be who we are."

"Everything's gonna be fine." She said it like she didn't believe it. "That's all I told him."

Jeremy watched his mom the whole time. The bored expression on his face never changed.

"That all you said?"

"Yeah." Theresa looked almost calm but her face was tight.

"When's Dust get here?"

"I don't know if he ever does."

A thick dark arm swooped through Vollmer's line of vision and a hand slapped her cheek hard. She fell back, away from Jeremy.

"Wrong answer." He leaned in, a black man, the voice soft. "He's coming, right?"

"I," Theresa caught her breath, "don't know. He wrote down the address."

"He never said meet you here?"

"He wrote this address and Keene's name. He talked about a girl down south."

"Girl or woman?"

Theresa tilted her head.

The man asked again. "If he balled her, would it be kiddy rape?"

"Oh," Theresa said. Now that the question was ugly she got it. "A woman."

"You get her name?"

"He said it, yeah. Val. Valerie, I think."

"Was he ballin' her?"

Theresa pressed her lips tight before she spoke. "He said he wasn't. I don't believe him."

The black man grinned. "And you said you don't know shit."

"That one's a guess."

"We want your guesses too," he said. "Where do you guess Valerie is? How far south?"

"A same day round trip. Monterey maybe. Hell, he coulda lied, she coulda been down the street or north."

"What's the boy know?" He took a step sideways in the child's direction.

Vollmer saw everything through his doorway across the hall, heard all but the occasional quiet word. The black guy would get everything he could from her, and when he didn't get enough one of the other guys would come in and do whatever they thought was necessary.

The black guy was pretty good, but what he got from her just now Rico already knew. If there was anything else to get, Vollmer had to be the one to get it. But not in this house right now, with a guy in front of him and at least two somewhere else he couldn't see.

Vollmer retreated toward the back of the house, away from this guy pointlessly threatening a woman and child, maybe hurting them. He could hurt them but he had to keep them alive in case they knew anything. In case he and Rico had been too subtle. He wouldn't make that mistake the next time he questioned them. When he took them away, alive would be all he needed. Everyone else here would be in no shape to follow, in no shape at all except for burial.

"He doesn't know anything!" Theresa shouted from the couch, Jeremy close beside her.

Tré leaned in, his face in Jeremy's. "Dust talked to you, right kid?"

"My name's Jeremy. You don't get to call me kid."

Tré pulled his head back. "Why? Did he?"

Jeremy nodded. "Dust taught me stuff. Guy stuff. Stuff my mom couldn't."

"Like what?" Tré asked. "How to fight?"

"Other stuff too," Jeremy said. "What a man does."

"What's a man do?"

"He takes care of people," Jeremy said. "He doesn't wait to be asked."

"Like he's taking care of you now? Like he ran out on you?"

"Uncle Dust had something to do. He said sometimes he's an asshole. I don't believe him."

"You got a lotta faith," Tré said, "in the man who put you in this mess."

"Uncle Dust didn't do this. You guys did."

"Nah," Tré said. "Your belief in the man is heart-warming, kid, but it's misguided. Dust disappeared because the mess is all his. That's the way that goes. And he told your mom enough to put you in the mess too. We don't know what he told you, what he told your mom, but if he didn't do nothin', we wouldn't have to know. It's on him. We ain't done shit. Only shit bein' done is if you two don't answer our questions."

"I don't know where he went," Jeremy said. "I don't know why. I think he got in trouble. It wasn't his fault."

"That man didn't just make the trouble," Tré said. "He dumped it on y'all." He looked at Theresa. "You're in a pile of shit. You ready to get out from under?"

"I told you," she said. "We told you. All we know. We told you all we know."

Stone got into the back yard easily. He'd reconned the house enough, the back was the only way in that wouldn't get him shot. He wasn't giving up and returning to the car. Instead he listened through the back door that led into the kitchen. They talked soft, he couldn't hear the words, then a door opened, had to be the one that led to the living room. He waited a couple minutes to be sure. Nothing but silence so he pushed the door open slow, stepped behind it into the kitchen and reached inside his jacket.

He got the Glock in his hand just in time to see the tall man in the plaid shirt standing in the kitchen with a Walther PPK aimed at his chest.

"The hand comes out empty," the tall man said.

Stone held onto the Glock, kept it in his jacket. "The hand don't come out." The guy with the Walther wouldn't want gunshots. Too loud.

The tall man nodded. "Into the kitchen."

The tall man waved him in and he took two steps forward, just inside the kitchen, stopped beside the refrigerator. A man appeared from behind the fridge with a long knife. The blade caught him in the neck and stopped the hitch in his stride, turned it into a brief spasm.

He screamed but only a moment as the knife came out of him fast and slashed across his throat. The sound as he fell was a gurgle. He hit the floor and the man who stabbed him stuffed a rag in his mouth and stepped back. He barely moved as he bled out.

"Good job keeping him quiet," Willis said. "Now you gotta lose him."

"Lose?" Platt was a lot more dangerous than bright.

"Can't leave him here, can't let them see." Willis

tipped his head toward the front of the house. "Can't leave blood on the floor."

Platt bunched his eyes together, shook his head.

"Bag the motherfucker so he don't bleed on no more floors, take him into the big bathroom, throw him in the tub. Then cut him up. The usual. But before they," Willis aimed a thumb at the front of the house, "come in here, this floor gotta be scrubbed good enough they don't see no blood."

"Fool the cops that way too."

"Cops ain't comin' here," Willis said. "Got no reason."

"Better be sure about that," Platt said. "You're in the room too."

They both looked at the dead man on the floor.

"And it's a Keene house," Willis said. "During this war, a lotta places might get raided. You're right, Platt."

Platt looked surprised.

"You get done with the body," Willis said, "we're gone. Burn this place down. Let forensics go through the ashes."

Platt crossed the room, opened the cabinet under the kitchen sink. He grabbed a couple of large trash bags from a box, walked back to the dead man. "Gimme a hand?"

Willis joined him. "You lift the body, I'll pull the bag over."

Platt got his arms under the corpse's upper torso, lifted him. Willis pulled the bag down over his head as far as it would go.

"Now the feet," Willis said, but he saw the problem already. The dead man wasn't that tall, but the bags were too short. Platt lifted the corpse's lower half and

Willis brought the second bag as high as it went but there was a good-sized gap in the middle. "Fuck."

"What?"

Willis looked at Platt. Dumb as he was, he had to see the problem. Apparently not. "Motherfucker's too tall. Gotta cut him some before you move him."

Platt shrugged. "They was outta the tall bags when I went to the store. I'll bring the tools down here."

"No!" Willis spent too much energy not letting Platt's stupidity piss him off. Didn't really work, just made the anger show in bursts. He bit his lower lip, sighed. "First we find a way so the blood in here don't get too bad. Don't wanna freak out our guests. Already too scared to talk." He stopped to think and Platt just stopped. Willis knew he was alone on the thinking. Like Platt was alone on touching the dead man.

Keene walked the house as he talked on the phone, steadiest exercise he got. The house's windows had been replaced by walls. Windows were for regular houses, where it was okay to see and be seen. What had been de-signed as a living room was his war room, one map on a wall and another on its long table. The map on the wall showed his and Lee's territories as they were, the one on the table as he wanted them to be. As they would be when the war ended. He expected it to take a year.

Keene was comfortable walking dark rooms, giving commands without looking at his maps. He knew where everyone was and where they should be. There were times to withdraw and times to attack. Never fight an even fight.

Lee's people were well-trained too, but Keene played

this like chess, saw the next several moves. And unless Lee was brilliant in a way he hadn't shown, or had reinforcements Keene didn't know about, the war should break the way Keene wanted. Provided all his commands were executed exactly.

It was a nice neighborhood, but not rich. Rico looked at Carelli. "Thought Keene was a player."

"You want to see money well spent," Carelli smiled, "fuck with him."

Rico found street parking end of the block. "Come on." He got out of the car.

Carelli didn't argue. Probably wasn't used to having a gun pulled on him, but he knew how to respond.

Not a lot of property in front of the house. Two tall, solid-looking guys in suit coats outside the front door, coats that no doubt covered heavy artillery.

"Subtle." Rico turned up the walkway, Carelli beside him. They stopped when they reached the guards.

"What?" one said.

"Carelli and Rico to see Keene," Carelli said.

The guard held a button on the door. "Say it again."

Carelli spoke louder. "Carelli and Rico to see Keene."

No one answered. They waited. Looked at the guards, the guards looked back. Nothing either way. Five minutes. The door buzzed, opened from the inside.

"In," a deep voice said.

Carelli entered, Rico followed. The man in the front hall was seven feet tall and built like a Greek god. "Against the wall," he said, the same deep voice.

Rico spoke as he turned. "One on the shoulder, one on the hip."

The giant took both pistols in one hand, the other hand on Rico's back. "Nice." He emptied both magazines quickly, handed the guns back to Rico.

Rico holstered his now useless pistols. Carelli didn't get frisked. The giant returned his attention to the front door as two more guards joined them and walked Rico and Carelli down a corridor and into a room where a short man sat at a beautiful round oak table. Three chairs available. He nodded at two and Rico and Carelli sat.

"Carelli," the short man said, his voice high pitched. He looked at Rico, his voice the same pitch and tone, no question in his words. "And Rico. You work for Tenny. You want a man named Dust."

Rico nodded. "Yeah. Keene?"

No answer to that, like it wasn't a question but an acknowledgment. No change in the man's expression. "You came to me. What do you want?"

"I got guys outside a house at 2731 Hunter. That yours?"

Keene shrugged. "I'd have to check the address. What I don't have is Dust. If I did you could have him."

Rico nodded. Keene might not fear Tenny, but it didn't make sense for a man at war to piss off another man with soldiers. "I need to know about that address. If it's Dust inside, we're goin' in. If it ain't—well, we might be goin' anyway."

Keene hooked a finger at one of his guards. The man stepped forward and leaned down. Keene whispered in his ear. The man left the room. "We'll know in a few minutes."

Rico didn't nod, didn't thank Keene either. If it was a Keene house, the part about going in anyway was a threat. Rico figured a threat was the fastest way to an answer. "You know Dust." He said it casual.

"A lotta years back," Keene said. "Good worker. Didn't leave trails."

Dust was weird like that. Left all his marks on his personal life. "He did his last job dirty. Owes Tenny."

"How much did he take?"

"More than his life's worth."

Keene stood, raised his palms from the table and pressed his weight on his fingers so they stretched and turned red. "That could mean he took a penny."

Carelli smiled wide.

Rico's face stayed grim, fucking sick of people thinking business was funny. "What he took could get shared if someone helped find the bastard. I'm here for him."

Keene's hands came off the table, hung gently at his sides. He looked relaxed but prepared to strike.

The guard who'd left the room returned, walked straight to Keene, whispered in his ear. Keene whispered something back, listened to the answer. He waved toward the wall and the man went back there. A feminine gesture, it reminded Rico of Camila, a quiet girl he lived with awhile until she shot him twice in the arm with a .22.

A large desk stood against the wall behind Keene. He turned to it, opened a tall drawer, and removed three stacked glasses and a bottle, wiped the glasses with a cloth and filled them. He set a glass in front of Rico and another in front of Carelli, came back with the third glass. "Yamazaki." He sat. "Japanese whisky. A personal favorite."

Carelli took a drink, grinned as though appreciative.

Rico stared at his glass then at Keene. "What the fuck he tell you?"

Keene drank, set his glass on the table, leaned forward, and talked soft. And high, always high. "Your men should pull away from that house. It's one of mine, and it's critical."

"Critical for us, too," Rico said. "We ain't pullin' away."

Keene looked at Rico, as though to measure him. Good men don't measure easy. "The men I got there," Keene said, "yours go in, they won't come out."

Rico looked Keene in the eyes. "You don't know who I got."

"Don't matter," Keene said.

"And if one of mine went in?" Rico asked.

"And pulled a weapon on my men? He's dead."

"My guy has a Glock and he's good."

Keene shook his head. "My men have stealth. You shoulda come to me first."

Rico drank until his glass was empty, set the glass down, and glared at Keene. "What about the girl? And the kid?"

"What?" Keene looked surprised.

"The girl Dust left. She went to that house. That's why we're there. Your guys let her in."

"MotherFUCK." Keene's eyes bulged at the guard who'd whispered to him. "Bring me a goddamn phone." Keene finished his glass, walked back to the desk, poured himself another with his back to the table and drank it in a slug.

Keene waved to the guard still on the wall, pointed at Rico and Carelli. "Take them outta here."

Rico stood without urging, glared at the guard, and walked to the door, Carelli in front of him.

The door shut behind them.

* * *

Tré yelled from the living room. "Willis!"

Willis charged through the door from the kitchen into the living room. The woman and her kid sat still on the couch. Willis glared at Tré, tipped his chin in Theresa and Jeremy's direction. "You said my fucking name."

Tré held out his cell phone. "I won't say his."

Willis grabbed the phone, spoke into it. "Yeah."

It was Keene, and he was pissed. When did the girl get there, when was he gonna find out. Why did he have to call Tré, why couldn't he call Willis. Willis held the phone away from his ear. Keene hit high notes, stopped to draw breath.

Willis talked fast. "She said your name. I figure anyone knows the house is yours, we wanna talk. So we brought her in. Saw this guy watching right away, then he's joined by two more guys. The other guys leave pretty fast, then he rolls on us. Alone. That's why my phone's off, we had to keep quiet a minute. So we dealt with the guy. Still dealing, was gonna give you a call. From a better phone. Ain't had time."

"You had a visitor?"

"Surprise guest got surprised."

"Permanent?"

"Yeah."

Keene exhaled like a hiss. "You got your next hole planned when you crawl out of this?"

"You know where. You're gonna lose this one."

"Lose?"

"Only way to clean this place is get rid of it."

A second of silence then Keene spoke again. "I want Dust as soon as he shows."

161

"I'll call when there's news."

"Do this so it's worth it. Call me from the next place." Keene ended the call.

Willis walked back to Tré, handed him the phone with one hand and punched him in the gut with the other. Tré bent forward and Willis punched him in the head. Tré was tough, stood there staggered.

"Don't say my name." Willis walked back to the kitchen.

One stranger comes to town and all this shit...A dead man—maybe Rico's best man—and Keene's men killed him. And those men had one hell of a mess to clean.

Keene drummed his fingers on the table, stood, stretched, turned to the desk behind him, and grabbed his bottle, poured two fingers and put the bottle away. A couple hundred dollars a bottle, that didn't bother him, but bottles sure went a lot faster during a war. He picked up the glass and, still standing, looked at the door Rico had walked through. Rico's man was dead and Keene moved that way. He didn't want Rico or, worse, Tenny, to side with Lee. A war is best fought on as few fronts as possible. Keene stared at that door, no one coming through it now. He lifted his glass, drank with his head thrown back and eyes closed.

Rico and Carelli were brought back to the room, one armed guard behind them, the other already on the wall. Carelli sat as before. Rico stood just inside the door, ignored everyone but Keene. "Vollmer?"

Keene looked at Rico from his chair, his face relaxed,

voice stern. "You want another drink?"

"Fuck that." He didn't sit down or step forward, just stood there.

"You need to call your guys off that house. No one's gonna wanna be there soon."

"What about Vollmer?"

"If he's the guy went in, he ain't comin' out."

Rico's face went blank. "Fuck. I told him don't go in." His usual grim look returned. "But if somethin' looked wrong…"

"It's my house," Keene said. "We're at war. We don't take chances."

"Fuck," Rico said again, not blank anymore, angry now. "Fuck."

"It's war," Keene said. "Sometimes we lose good soldiers. We're on the same side."

"Yeah?" Rico cocked his head, somewhere between a question and a threat.

"You want Dust, I'm glad to help. Money's always good, favors can be better."

"What kinda deal we talkin'?"

"We get Dust," Keene said, "we get the money. Tenny got somethin' to trade, he talks to me."

Rico nodded. "The guys I got coming…" He hesitated. "Ain't as good as who I had here."

"Ain't as good as who I got. You," he leered at Rico, "you could make it here, I heard about you. I got East Bay soldiers. Been in wars their whole lives. A little softer down south."

Rico sighed, a sound he rarely made. "Vollmer wasn't soft."

"He went at the wrong guys," Keene said. "My people, my turf? Talk about home field advantage." Keene laughed.

Rico sat down and laid his massive palms on the table.

Carelli had watched the whole scene. He pulled his chair back in.

Keene leaned forward, eyes on Rico. "Every man with power thinks he knows what it is. Until he steps up in class and sees the real thing. This part of California, you ain't seeing more power than what you see right now. Me and Lee, we got the best soldiers, but he made a move on me. He's gonna learn how a war is fought. You ain't goin' that far."

Rico looked confused, tried to cover it with calm. "I go where I want."

"You don't want much. Dust. I wouldn't give a fuck, but he's a profit item now."

Rico glared. "So could we find him and shut up?"

Keene burst from his chair, leaned across the table, and backhanded Rico hard. Rico's head snapped back. Before he could react guards pushed his shoulders down.

Keene stared down at him from across the table. "Work for me or get the fuck outta my town."

Rico brought a hand to his chin, brushed the slapped cheek with a thumb, eyes on Keene. "Must be Vollmer fuckin' with my head." He turned to Carelli. "You been paid and the work ain't done. Find Dust. Like you said, your word is your life."

Carelli talked to everyone. No one saw Dust since Mimi said she did. She said he was looking for Keene. If he was, he coulda found him by now.

Carelli preferred gathering information on pay phones but, despite his small stature, he was capable of as much physical cruelty as necessary. A short drive to Oakland, but it was away from the action he cared about. He drove 75 on the freeway where the limit was 65, then 35 on surface streets where the limit was 25 or 30. Nothing he'd get pulled over for. And Mimi would tell him what he needed to know fast. For her sake, it better be fast enough. Carelli didn't give a fuck about her sake, only he'd make her best interests coincide with his. One difference—didn't matter to him if she survived.

Carelli drove to Oakland Chinatown.

Rico's phone buzzed in his pocket. He straightened enough to pull it out, looked at the number then at Keene. "I gotta take this."

"Talk here."

It was the best answer Rico could hope for. "Yeah?" he said into the phone.

The voice on the other end gave him the names he wanted: guys who were on the way, guys who should be here by now. Rico already knew about some of them, was glad to hear about the others. Even with Keene in the room, Rico had to ask. "They all know to check in with Vollmer when they get here?"

"Yeah."

"I wanna know who talked to him and when. Call me back. Soon." Rico pushed a button, pocketed his phone.

"You got hope," Keene said.

"He wouldn't die easy," Rico said. "Don't care how good your guys are."

"One mistake," Keene said. "All it takes."

"Vollmer don't make mistakes."

* * *

Platt had a flattened cardboard box under the dead man's ass, plastic trash bags around his head and feet. He carried the dead man careful, one arm under each end of the cardboard, hoped any new blood spills came out on that and not the floor. Not that it mattered so much if they were torching the joint, only Willis wanted it to look nice for the guests. Like they'd live long enough to swear to anything.

He carried the corpse across the floor to where the counter had been cleared on both sides of the sink. The sink was split into two sides with a tile barrier between. One side to wash, one to rinse, but that wasn't how this would work.

No way he could do this in his own kitchen, the dead fucker was too long. Platt hadn't known he'd have to kill someone here, or that he'd have to cut up the body so they could get rid of it but, the way he worked, it always made sense to have his tools and plastic and drop cloths with him. He set them up before he moved the body—covered every cabinet and wall with plastic sheets, covered everything else with drop cloths. Platt laid the corpse's lower back, cardboard beneath, on the tile barrier. The rest of the corpse extended across the sink and counter in either direction. He lifted one of the sheets enough to plug in the chain saw and went to work at the sink.

Power tools roared from the other end of the house. Theresa didn't know what the hell was going on. And the black guy who was watching her and Jeremy—what was up with him and the guy who beat the shit out of him because the black guy said the white guy's name? Fucking gangsters, what did they think she'd witnessed? Or was that just general principle? Or were they mad because Dust fucked them over for money? And they thought she knew where Dust was or that he might come for her.

If the gangsters were waiting for Dust, Theresa figured they had a long wait ahead. But she hoped they were right. Dust would show up, pay whatever he owed, and they'd let everyone go. Unlikely as that was, hope was all she had. But what if he owed more than money? What if he came here and tried to work a deal and it didn't work? They didn't seem like people. She wrapped her arm tighter around Jeremy and—Goddammit—if they did something to Jeremy, what would she do?

Tré stood across from the woman and child. Willis joined them. "So," Willis said, and stepped toward the couch where the two of them sat, "what's your name?"

"Theresa."

He looked at the boy. "And you?"

"His name's Jeremy," Theresa said.

Willis nodded at the protective mother. His eyes stayed with hers. "And you got this address from Dust? That motherfucker never talked."

Theresa shook her head. "The address was on a scrap of paper. He left in a hurry."

Willis smiled. "Most women glad to see that man go."

"I didn't come for him. I came to see Keene." Theresa sat straight the whole time, never leaned forward or back. She wore jeans and running shoes and never crossed her legs, just sat in attentive classroom pose.

Willis hadn't really looked at her before. She was pretty, sure, but she had attitude. Without getting out of hand with it, at least so far. He stood with his hands at his sides, his shirt hanging over the top of his jeans, his pistol behind him in a holster on his hip. He tried to look comfortable, knew comfort wasn't possible for her right now. "I know Dust. Been a few years."

"And you know Keene?"

"The name," Willis said. "Everybody knows that name."

"But you guys know more than the name."

Willis nodded. He supposed he'd given away that much. "He's not a man anyone with sense looks for. So I understand why Dust would look for him. But you? You're better off home, whatever happens there."

"They threatened to kill us at home."

"They wouldn't, though." Willis shook his head. "Dust came up here. Anyone dies, it's gonna be here. You shoulda stayed home."

"You lettin' us go?"

"You shoulda stayed home."

Platt had cut the body up into dozens of pieces, easier to pack but it took hours. Dawn now. Sunlight coming, but would they slip out in it or in the dark? Either way they had to torch at least the kitchen. Willis said don't worry about that, he knew exactly how to burn what had to be burned.

Willis had always set fires. He'd gotten away with it as a teen through sheer luck. As he grew up he got good enough to get paid for it, learned from real pros when he got busted and spent a couple years inside. The more he was paid, the better he had to be. Until he got so good that even Keene paid him to burn places down, fires where any evidence that Keene was involved would get Willis killed.

The fire would catch the neighborhood off guard. The point of this block was to be in the middle of nothing. Keene had the house for years, wouldn't like losing it. But everything dies when it's time.

Keene wouldn't have planned on things going wrong, but it sure looked like he'd allowed for the possibility.

Platt wrapped his packages one by one, like Christmas presents. Christmas presents for dogs. Meat and bones, the perfect gift. He wedged as many packages as he could into a travel bag, started another. Didn't matter how many bags it took, every package would find its way to a different dog.

Willis sent Tré out to wait with Theresa and Jeremy in her Jetta while Platt took his suitcases down to his car. Willis was the last one in the house, checking for anything that might be incriminating. The fire had to look like an accident, not a crime scene.

Theresa had brought her own car, it couldn't be left to be discovered and investigated. It worked better this way; Platt could leave on his own, alone as he fed body parts to whatever dogs he found.

Willis finished his search of the house. They'd done well, no evidence that would survive the blaze. The fire was going slowly for now. A kitchen fire, it would burst into flames that would consume everything (but mainly the kitchen floorboards, and fast). By then, he and the rest would be long gone.

He stepped outside, Platt's car already gone and no other sign of life but the people waiting in the Jetta. No one to notice everyone leaving the house at once. Willis locked the front door and shut it behind him then stepped down the stairs to join Tré and their hostages.

Theresa sat behind the wheel. The tall man—Willis, the name she wasn't supposed to know—joined her in the front. The black man with the scar sat in back with Jeremy.

"Where we goin'?" Theresa's voice barely trembled, like she couldn't let these guys know they scared her.

"Straight," Willis said. "Drive the speed limit. I tell you when to turn."

"What kind of place? Another house? A hotel?"

"A hiding place. But this time, the man gonna set us free."

Theresa didn't know what he meant or why they wanted her to drive, guessed maybe it looked least suspicious. Her in front with the tall man, Jeremy in back with the other man, like a half ugly family outing. The men by themselves would look like a criminal conspiracy.

It was easy to drive the crowded Jetta the speed limit so long as they stayed off the freeway. Theresa's foot pressed the gas a little farther to the floor than usual; the damn thing didn't like to go fast.

"Left at the next corner."

Theresa turned where she was told. She only wanted out of this alive. She and Jeremy hadn't done anything, but these men didn't want to hear that. The man who threatened her and Jeremy in their apartment sure hadn't cared. He'd still be after her even if these men let her go. Or maybe the only way they'd let her go was if something happened that convinced not only them, but Rico and everyone else who gave a shit. When something happened, not if. It had to be when.

She held back tears, had to look strong for Jeremy and these men. Had to act like she didn't give a fuck, but if she talked much they'd know. Still, she should probably say something. "We going far before I turn again?"

"Only one lane, whatta you care?" The tall man didn't make it easy.

"Just talkin'," she said.

"Easin' the tension?"

She sensed him looking at her, glanced his way.

He wore a big smile, bigger than his teeth merited. "We like the tension," he said.

She'd try not to make that mistake again, got her eyes back on the road. "It's not like we came up here to be tourists. I just don't know Berkeley. Want the drive to go smooth as possible."

"Stay straight 'til I tell you to turn, you don't gotta know shit. Except what else you remember about Dust."

"He took something, right?" Theresa said. "Or you guys wouldn't give a fuck. Probably money, or something worth money. Do I look rich to you?"

"You look scared."

"My mom ain't scared of you guys," Jeremy said. He was a little old for that kind of faith in his mother, but his voice sounded small enough.

"Shut up, kid," the tall man said.

"Don't talk to my son like that."

"Fuck you, bitch. And fuck your kid."

Theresa took a deep breath, probably visible, but she didn't do a damn thing, just drove straight. She hoped something went wrong and somehow this man died. She'd never wanted to see a man die before. In his case, she'd make an exception.

The fast lane wasn't fast enough but Cobb couldn't get pulled over. Not with the woman lying on his back seat who, although under a blanket, had obviously been beaten up. Beaten badly enough that Cobb was afraid she might die from the lousy ventilation if he put her in the trunk. He didn't want her dead yet.

Cobb didn't pray same as he didn't beg, but he sure hoped he didn't hit traffic, hoped he found Dust in the East Bay. Berkeley was a good place for a white man to disappear—like Oakland for damn near any race that wasn't white—but Cobb was a tracker, damn good at finding men who lost themselves.

Exile on Main Street in the CD player. It was his favorite hunting album, about the perfect length for this drive without traffic. He wouldn't hit traffic. He couldn't hit traffic. He was gonna find Dust in Berkeley and he was gonna kill Dust in Berkeley. And if he didn't find the money Dust stole, he'd make sure Tenny knew who to pay for killing the bastard.

Olivia lay on the car's back seat, doped but not quite asleep, although nowhere near mobile. She wished she slept. Instead she wondered who this man was if he didn't work for Rico. Was the whole world looking for

Dust? Someone had to know where he went, every psycho couldn't be counting on her.

But now that she'd seen his face, would this man let her live? How could she escape? She couldn't even move. She lay conscious, wished there was peace in sleep, but it didn't matter, sleep wouldn't come. Peace wouldn't come. This man had hurt her and would probably hurt her more, then he would kill her. But only after he'd made her suffer so much he was certain of her ignorance.

How he wasn't already certain was beyond her. How much more she could suffer was beyond her. She wished all of this was beyond her. But she was here, and nothing lay beyond. Unless someone saved her. More likely, her savior would be death.

Cobb got to Oakland on the freeway, Berkeley was next. That's where Keene was based. Cobb didn't know where, but he knew there was nice housing north of University Avenue. He had a feeling the place he wanted wouldn't be up in the hills. There was a University exit, he'd get off there.

The corpse-to-be on the back seat would wake up soon. For now she was quiet. Cobb hoped she stayed that way.

He got off the freeway, emerged on an end of University that was ugly nothing. He drove down it, got to ugly something. Progress. But even outside a dive bar, a beat-to-hell woman couldn't be seen on his back seat. Cobb knew a place with parking in back. The lot was down a dirt path that looked like an alley except for the missing dumpster and junkies. His silver 2015 Impala wasn't the slimmest car around, but it fit down the path with inches to spare on either side. He got to the back of the building. The lot was close to full, but there was a space in the back row. He turned the car and backed into the space so the Impala faced out, its trunk as close to the wall as he could get it.

The bar had a back door. Cobb would have to keep an eye on anyone who left that way. He opened the door and walked in, looked for a familiar face. There were a few who could be here. He approached the bar slow, looked at everyone he passed long enough to rule them out, walked to the front and took a stool that faced the back door.

After a minute the bartender approached, a bulky man gone soft, beer gut and thinning gray hair that drooped to his shoulders. "What'll it be?" he asked, like it was an effort to finish the question.

"Got any Mexican beers?"

"Dos Equis in a bottle."

"Gimme one a those," Cobb said. "Hey, Muzzy been in today?"

"Don't know no Muzzy." The bartender turned away. Unless this was his first day here, he knew Muzzy. Hell, maybe even then.

Cobb had a twenty on the bar when the bartender came back. "I ain't a cop."

"Nah." The bartender picked up the twenty, looked at Cobb in his sport coat and buttoned shirt. Nothing fancy but not too shabby. "You look more like what they call, uh, a private dick." A couple guys nearby laughed as the bartender walked away. He put the money in the register opposite the middle of the bar, came back and laid a ten and six ones on the bar. "The beer's four bucks."

Cobb let the money lie there. He supposed the bartender used to be a tough guy, still thought he was. "Muzzy, Seth, Dash, Duane. You gonna tell me you don't know none of 'em?"

"I don't know no one, don't wanna. That includes you." The bartender talked loud enough they had an audience.

Cobb wasn't here to be noticed but really didn't give a fuck if he was. So long as they left his car alone. "Look, fat boy, I ain't doin' nothin' to bring cops here. That's the kinda dick I am. I ain't gonna wreck your bar or do nothin' else that makes you show whatever piece you got behind the bar. And if you got a record, it's longer than mine. I done a lotta things, one thing I ain't done is get caught." He drank from his bottle, kept a hand on its neck. "I don't know who you know, but I guarantee I'm the most dangerous motherfucker you ever saw." He looked at the bartender with narrow, cold steel eyes, gave the same look to a couple of big old boys this end of the bar. "All those guys I mentioned," he looked back at the bartender, "they gonna be damn grateful you don't know 'em. 'Til they find out it was Cobb askin'. Get holda Muzzy now. Tell him it's Cobb, tell him I asked about his black Vincent, tell him I said get his ass down here." He pushed the sixteen dollars toward the bartender. "And keep the fuckin' change."

Keene turned from his seat beside the driver and looked at Rico in the back, a gunman on either side. "We're goin' now where they should, no guarantees. We didn't talk addresses over the phone."

"Understood," Rico said.

"That old house went up, I hear. No one there by now but fire trucks and cops."

"I left messages," Rico said, like there was a question. "With all my guys. No one picked up."

"Good policy," Keene said.

Rico looked worried. "Policy's good. Reasons might not be."

"A lotta guys take one chance too many."

"But if it's Vollmer," Rico said, "there's a reason he took the chance. I wanna know why."

"Maybe we find out," Keene said. "Maybe not."

Dogs in Berkeley weren't so easy to find, but Oakland? Everybody had a fucking dog. Lotta pits behind fences, thick iron, cheap tin, whatever, wooden slatted shit that looked ready to fall. Platt didn't need neighborhoods so bad the dogs might get out. Not that the dogs scared him, just anyone fucked up enough to own a dog like that and give it an easy way out of the yard might be fucked up enough to shoot him through a living room window. He didn't need some high security place with dogs either; a car pulling up to a place like that might attract attention. That's where the Oakland suburbs came in—not suburbs by a lot of standards, but people trying to live middle-class lives in a city where it wasn't far from the middle to the depths.

Platt drove slow, windows down, listened for dogs, looked for signs. Not "Beware of Dog" signs, any idiot could put one of those up, but signs that a place actually had big dogs in it. If he threw a package over a fence and anyone noticed the flesh was human—he didn't think he'd get caught, but it couldn't be good getting seen. Better if he saw a metal fence with a few big dogs behind it, tossed several bags over and got out fast. Once those dogs tore into the bags, however much noise they made no one would slow them down. And Platt would be on to the next house.

He'd used this strategy before. It was fast, efficient. He pulled around a corner and saw three German Shepherd/God-knows-what mixes, big teeth bared and barking loud at a white woman walking with a child on a tricycle and two small dogs. The helmeted child seemed oblivious to the sounds, and the woman walked steadily, restraining her yappy little rodent dogs from scurrying off.

On the opposite side of the street, Platt drove slowly down the hill. The woman and her little beasts were off the block when he made his U-turn at the stop sign at the bottom. The big dogs were just before the corner at the top of the hill. Platt pulled over right in front of the driveway they guarded. The angry beauties barked at him as he got out of the car and opened the trunk full of meat. Platt grabbed three packages in each hand and stopped a couple feet outside the gate. The dogs kept barking but they drooled now, their eyes alert. He wished he had time to stay for the fun, he'd have grabbed a fourth bag in each hand and watched the fight. He smiled at the dogs, damn near drooled himself as he tossed the wrapped meat packages over the gate. When he'd thrown three and all the dogs were farther away, he tossed the other three through the gaps in the gate, right up the middle where they might fight over them. Might not happen here but sometimes with strays they'd fight over a piece of meat and one would get into the other's throat and keep going. Get that piece of meat then the other.

Platt loved dogs.

Cobb was at the bottom of his second bottle of Dos Equis when Muzzy came in, his face looking like he'd worn it too long.

"Tired, Muzz?"

Muzzy took the stool beside him and then some. He was fat, about forty, and looked like his life was fucked. "This bitch," he said, and waved to the bartender.

"Girlfriend?" Cobb said.

"I'm used to the wife," Muzzy said. "Fuck her, you know, and she feels the same. And 'til death do we part."

"I got this," Cobb said, when the bartender got there. "Another of these for me. Muzzy?"

Muzzy's eyes widened a little at the thought of free drinks. "A double shot of Jack," he said. "And a Heineken."

"No wonder you're so fucked up, Muzzy," Cobb said, as the bartender turned away. "You can't even order a good drink."

"Fuck you, Cobb."

"Don't say that loud," Cobb said. "I ain't here."

Muzzy wasn't some punk, he just acted like one sometimes. He nodded.

Cobb had two new twenties on the bar to greet their drinks when they arrived. "Keep it," Cobb said, and the bartender picked them up.

The bartender knew enough not to bother saying thank you. Cobb wanted him the fuck out of there and he was out.

Cobb drank from his beer while Muzzy downed half his double shot.

Cobb spoke as they set their drinks down. "Fuck your problems, Muzzy." He opened his wallet, held out a hundred-dollar bill. "Tell me where Keene is."

"For that?" Muzzy looked at Cobb like he was crazy. "I need five times that."

"You get double."

"For where he usually is, or his safe houses too?" Muzzy said. "There's a war goin' on."

"You sayin' he left the main place?"

"Don't know shit for sure. He got the backups for a reason, though. If he gotta move? That's where he goes."

"How many places we talkin'?"

"Three. His place plus two."

"Gimme all three," Cobb said. "You get five."

"Stop here," Keene said, and his driver pulled over. Keene looked back at Rico. "That car across the street—hers?"

Rico had already seen the Jetta, didn't need to look again. "Same as at the other house."

"So, the guys inside are waiting for the other car."

"Other car?"

"The one my guys drove."

"Could be in the garage," Rico said.

"Not what that garage is used for."

Rico nodded. Didn't matter what was stored there. "What are we waiting for?"

"I wanna see who else shows up."

"If you don't trust me," Rico said, "why you gonna

sit out in the open like this?"

Keene grinned. Didn't make him look happy. "You coulda told your guys to storm the next place my guys go to. You wouldn't say shoot up the car you're in."

"So we sit here and wait 'til something goes wrong?"

"If I'm wrong and it goes wrong here," Keene said, "we clear out. And you die. If I'm right, I wanna be here when the good news comes."

Rico raised his eyebrows. "You think Dust is gonna show?"

"Word's out the right places. He cares about the girl, I hope."

Rico's turn to grin. "Dust is in this world for himself, nobody else. Don't even seem to like himself that much."

"And if word got out showing up was his best way to stay alive?"

"He'd try to think of a worse way."

ACT 5

A block from the meeting place, meat disposed of, Platt entered the intersection slow. He wanted to pull over in front of the new safe house but there was a dark sedan parked across the street. Other cars parked on the street but he didn't trust that sedan, needed proof it was empty. He took a left instead of going straight. No good approach from the rear but he wouldn't take the front not knowing who watched. His phone in his hand, he was about to call Willis—but who was in the car, and how did they know about this house unless Willis told them? Platt put the phone down, drove to the corner and made a right. The blocks were long, he could circle. But was the sedan extra security or were they taking him out? Didn't make sense, unless the guy he killed at the last house was someone who mattered. A war going on, strangers in town, that motherfucker could be anyone. Fuck. If he just had Keene's number. Willis did, and he had Willis's, but he couldn't trust Willis on this. Shit, if he was the fall guy, maybe he couldn't trust Keene. Couldn't play it like that, though. If he couldn't trust Keene he was dead no matter what. If it was just Willis it wasn't even a worry, only a man to kill.

But maybe it was none of that. A nice sedan was

parked across the street from the backup house, maybe it was safe to park in front and go in. Right. Maybe it was safe to show your back to armed strangers. He was fucking tired.

Platt circled halfway around the block and made a U-turn, came back about where he'd been, swung a left and pulled up behind the parked sedan. He opened his door as he parked, leapt out SIG Sauer .45 in hand, ran up and dropped belly down on their trunk, pistol pointed at their rear window. "Police!" he yelled. "Get out, y'all in back first, nothin' in your hands."

One bodyguard got out one side, the other out the other. Rico dropped to the floor of the back seat.

"You too!" Platt yelled. "Out slow, street side."

Rico got up, stepped out.

"You better be one a mine," a high voice said.

Platt hadn't heard the guy riding shotgun get out of the car, turned to the voice and saw a .38 aimed at his head. Platt kept his gun on one of the guards. "Police," he said. "Lower your weapon, sir."

"Fuck you," Keene said. "No one pulls up on my car on my block. Name's Keene. What's yours?"

Fuck. Even if the high-voiced man lied, he had the drop on him. "I'm Platt."

"Platt? Get in that fuckin' house with Willis and stop wastin' everyone's time."

Platt looked at the man ready to kill and crossed the street, walked to the front door.

"Back in the car," Keene said to his men and Rico.

Everyone got back in.

"Shit," Rico said, "Carelli said you can't even park long in Berkeley without gettin' noticed."

"Carelli," Keene said, "ain't got his own blocks."

Rob Pierce

Keene turned to the driver. "Let's go."

The engine started.

"That's your best guy?" Rico asked.

"Good man when he got someone givin' him orders."

"No way," Rico said. "No way a punk like that took Vollmer."

"No tellin' what happened that other house. But someone got took, and your guy's likely the guy."

Rico shook his head, in disbelief or convincing himself. "Vollmer's too smart for that fucking guy."

They pulled away from the curb.

"Back to your place?" Rico asked.

"A man's home is his castle," Keene said.

"It ain't my home." Rico's eyes switched from the armed thug on one side of him to the one on the other, then up to Keene.

"Mine either." Keene's upper lip twitched.

"And you want me with you while my guys look for Dust."

"They lookin' on my turf," Keene said. "They fuck with anything of mine, you're my ace in the hole."

"So we sit in that house and wait for news," Rico said.

"From my guys and from yours. Victory drinks when we win the war."

"Your war?" Rico asked.

"All the wars." Keene smiled. "We may stay dry awhile."

Platt entered the house and shut the door behind him, locked it. "We gotta talk."

"Yeah?" Willis looked at Platt, walked past their prisoners on the couch, left them with Tré. Platt walked

183

in a hurry. Willis joined him in the kitchen.

Platt shut the door as soon as they were inside. "A guy who says he's Keene's out front."

"He got the drop on you?"

"I pulled up on his car, had everyone to rights. He talked me out of it."

"He got the drop on you." Willis smiled.

"I thought he was Keene or he'd be dead!"

"What did he sound like?"

Platt looked confused.

"His voice," Willis said.

"High, but dangerous. Like a girl snake."

"That's Keene," Willis said. "So we ain't gotta worry about the house being watched."

A nicer living room, a nicer couch for Theresa and Jeremy to sit on at gunpoint. This place looked more like a real house than a getaway, furnished like someone actually lived here, but it didn't make a bit of fucking difference while the black man with the scar stood with that bigass pistol pointed at them.

"Could you put that down?" Theresa asked.

"Why? Scared?" The scarred man kept the pistol aimed at her belly.

Theresa sat taller, leaned forward like she might come at him.

"I like it," he said, "when you get your back up. What that saying means and the way you sit straight like that. Proud and sexy." He looked at Jeremy, shrugged. "Sorry, kid. Your mom looks good."

"I know she looks good," Jeremy said.

The man laughed. "You don't know the half of it."

He turned back to Theresa. "You know, though. You know what Dust liked. How he made money too, what he liked about that. Besides the money."

"I don't know what he did. Sometimes he'd go away for a while, come back with a lot of money, that's all. He did something else, probably hurt people. He never said what."

"He said all that and you never said shit? What else you holdin' back, bitch?"

"Hey!" Jeremy shouted.

The man turned the pistol on Jeremy. "Shut up, kid."

"Not him!"

He faced Theresa with the pistol again. "What'd he say about hurtin' people?"

"Never why," Theresa said.

"He talked to me, too," Jeremy said. "About what he did. He didn't say he hurt people. He said I should never loan money. Because I couldn't trust who gets it."

"What else?" the man asked.

"Never borrow," Jeremy said. "He said his job, he explained to people. How if they owed money and didn't pay, someone could take their house or their car."

"He explained that, huh?" The black man smiled, his teeth damn white.

"Yeah." Jeremy smiled back. "He helped them understand."

The man laughed. Theresa shuddered. Jeremy's smile vanished.

For Val, sex always led to disaster. That was why there were only four men she'd ever fucked. The fourth one was Rico. She still kinda hoped the thing with Rico could turn out good. Hell, she didn't even hope it, she just needed it. Needed someone to hold her without hurting her.

Dust was the first guy she'd slept with and they were teenagers at the time, so as pain went that breakup should barely count. Except it was first love, and she probably still loved him when she married Lucas. Dust didn't seem to give a fuck and Lucas acted like he adored her. No wonder she married him. He acted that way until shortly after Abram and Jesse were born. Then he left her. Bastard.

Not that Lucas could have done a goddamn thing about the third guy who fucked her. She didn't even know his name at the time. She found out later that he was called Peach, and he went to prison for rape and murder. Not for her rape, or Jesse and Abram's murders, but at least he did time. Less time than he was sentenced to, because Dust killed him in prison.

Then Dust came back to her. He was helping her and he needed her to help him. She did, and they slept together, then he was done with her, had a home to go to.

She'd never been the home anyone would go to. Not for long. When Dust came back to her again, she told him to fuck off.

And when Rico came to her and showed an interest, she thought he liked her. Didn't know she was just the means to an end. Fuck men. Fuck fucking. Fuck life.

A glass in her hand, Val ignored the rented movie on her TV. Waiting here wasn't safe. She drank. She had to get away from guys who cared about Dust. Move somewhere guys just liked a big woman. On good days when her face wasn't worn she was pretty enough, just fat. Some guys like fat. Maybe move up to Oakland. Black guys liked what she had, she'd seen the way they looked at her. They'd want to handle all of it.

Carelli reached Mimi's block. No parking so he extended his perimeter. A half mile away he found a tight space and paralleled into it. Not too tight a space if he could find a crane to get him out. He walked fast as he could around and through the crowds, several blocks of what felt like half the population of China. He was in a hurry among people who seemed to be accepting eternity.

The whole drive over he wondered how he'd get into Mimi's apartment. A little Mandarin worked fine when she was willing to see him. She wouldn't be so eager this time. Hell, he'd hit her then.

Carelli walked up the stairs to the front door, buzzed and had the same Mandarin exchange as before—Mrs. Fong managed the building, and years ago he'd kept quiet when cops asked about her nephew. He'd traded that silence for a lifetime of Chinatown gossip which, when it came from Mrs. Fong, was damningly accurate.

He charged into the building and up the stairs again. Elevator might be faster but he hated elevators, plus they didn't do a damn thing for his exercise regimen. Which already suffered from how much of his day was spent sitting down.

He reached Mimi's door, tried it. Locked. No way she'd let him in. The door might be easy enough to break through, if he was a thug like Rico. But he wasn't, or a burglar with B&E tools. His only way in would be verbal.

"Mimi," he said through the door. If she was inside she heard him, recognized his voice and would be wary.

He'd lie and she'd expect it. He had to tell a lie she wouldn't expect. He spoke in Mandarin. "Dust wants to see you. He knows you won't trust me. I'm going to him. I'm parked on 14th Street. Sidewalks are busy, you can follow me safe. Then I drive to him in Berkeley. Follow me in your car. When I reach the house I'll wait for you, show you where he is, you can see him yourself."

"Tell me the address," she said, from just inside the door.

"Twenty-nine thirty-one Hunter." Carelli walked away from her door to the stairs.

Downstairs near the entrance was too bare to be called a lobby. It was an entry and that was it, no furniture or plants. The keyed mailboxes were outside. There was one place to wait, the risk Carelli had to take, on the wall next to the elevator. He could see the front door from here, but it was wood, no window, no view outside. The first floor apartments were just a few feet away, but unless someone came through one of those doors, he could see no one and no one could see him.

The building was quiet. Carelli waited against the wall, his hands loose at his sides. A holstered pistol inside his coat but it would be stupid to hold it now. If anyone saw a white man by the elevator, he'd look suspicious even without a gun in his hand, but he wouldn't have to hurry away. If police came in, a strange man in a lobby without a gun would be a low priority for Oakland cops. With a gun? He'd have to make a break for it, those response times could be fast and violent.

Carelli waited impatiently but did his best to convey calm to his audience of none as he awaited Mimi's descent. If anyone were to see him, he was a white man out of place but that was all. A shame he was too short to be a cop. He pretty much dressed the part, but he doubted anyone would buy it.

The elevator door opened. Mimi stepped out and Carelli put a hand in her belly, pushed. She stumbled back into the elevator, fell on her ass. Carelli stepped in with her. The doors shut and he pressed the button for the top floor. Mimi looked up, fear on her face.

Carelli kicked her under the chin. Her head hit the back of the elevator.

"When's the last time you saw Dust?"

Her hand over her mouth. Blood on her fingers.

"This year?" he said. "Last year, five years ago?"

"T—today," she said.

Carelli kicked with his other foot, steadied himself. The old elevator kept rising. "Not when'd he call you and say what lies to tell. See him. When'd you fucking see him?"

She was pushed against the back wall of the elevator, blood streaming from her mouth as she struggled to sit up.

Carelli aimed his pistol at her head. "What did he say when he called?"

"He," she said, and swallowed. "He..." Words stopped coming, tears flowed.

Carelli holstered his pistol. "Let's go to your place." Nothing romantic, but right now, his kind of date. He helped Mimi to her feet, held her up, and at her floor walked her out the elevator and to her apartment.

The worn couch in her tiny living room was in a lot better shape than she was. Mimi plopped onto it, blood dripping from both sides of her mouth.

Carelli stood over her, a few feet back so she couldn't kick at him. The pistol remained holstered for now, out of sight. "You ain't my interest," he said. "Rather save the effort and not hurt you, but don't give a fuck if you suffer."

Mimi looked in his direction, too much pain on her face for anything else to show. "Dust was here. He left."

"Yeah, but what year? Y'see, Mimi, I know what you told us last time was bullshit. Maybe you still love Dust. God knows why, that man runs through women. But you lie about Dust? That's my problem. You know why? You wanna know why?" His hands came up from below his waist, his fingers semi-clenched. Mimi's eyes widened.

"Dust," Carelli said, "owes men who don't give a fuck who they hurt."

Carelli's pistol came out. He shot Mimi in the foot. She screamed.

He talked soft. "That's nothin' to what they do to me if I don't find him." He pointed the pistol at her other shoe. "When did you see Dust?"

"Years," she said, her voice a yelp.

"He called and gave you the lie."

"Yeah," she said.

"Gimme your phone."

Mimi had it in a case clasped to her hip. "Can I get a doctor?"

"Gimme the fucking phone or I shoot you in the head."

Mimi handed him the phone.

Carelli took it, made sure there weren't any land lines in the apartment, and walked away. "Call who you want."

* * *

Carelli looked at Mimi's call log as he walked back to the car. One call from Dust this morning, one call to Dust this afternoon, about the time Carelli and Rico left her. No text messages, no voice mails. What the hell—if Dust was that big an idiot, Carelli wouldn't be getting paid to find him.

It made no sense to tell Rico that Dust wasn't here. There was another bitch Dust might have gone to, but she was down near Monterey, he didn't know where. He wasn't far from the bus station. He drove there, parked, made phone calls, found out where she was and yeah Dust might be there. It was at least two hours away, but if Dust wasn't in Oakland, Carelli might as well go. Dust was there or he was gone. He was already gone from here. He wasn't coming back.

Carelli would come back. With answers, and they'd better be good enough that he could keep Rico's money.

Cobb parked outside Keene's. A couple of guards near the front door, no way to know who was inside. Cobb didn't have time to waste, didn't see how he could do anything here fast. No point in even trying this house. If Dust was in there, Keene wouldn't give him up.

He drove toward the first safe house. As he got close he started to cough. Turned into a fit. Goddamn air pollution. He rolled up his windows then noticed the smoke overhead. Not good. Sure enough, he got close to where he should turn and the street was blocked by cops. He glanced down that way. A fire truck outside a blazing house.

He kept going straight, headed for safe house number two. He was in a hurry and this was taking forever.

Fuck. He got there at last, parked across the street. He wanted to get close to the house, see what went on inside, but he had to be cautious. A backup house for Keene probably meant a place thugs went when shit at the main house went wrong, a place where murders could be kept secret. And the house they should be in was on fire. No way that was an accident.

Cobb's idea of caution meant he waited in the car a full minute before he got out. Several steps to the side and he saw the empty driveway with the closed garage door. Almost certainly locked and although the lock would be easier than going through the front door, Cobb had no way of knowing if the garage had a door that opened into the house. And if he broke into the garage during the day, he'd have to do it fast.

The front door would be watched. He watched it too as he walked straight ahead, hoped they didn't have enough men here to see the driveway from inside the house. The garage entrance looked electronic, nothing Cobb knew how to get past. A narrow gap between the garage and the house, he ducked into it and looked toward the back. Nothing but walls from here to there. He leaned against the house wall he'd started on and eased his head out to check the house, ready to return to his car. The front door opened. He pressed himself hard against the wall.

Cobb got his pistol out. He was frozen until someone came around that corner. Then they'd be dead. And he'd have to run and that would be a hard escape. He hoped he could move before then.

* * *

Olivia woke in a dark place, sore all over. It was hard to breathe. She turned on her side, hoped that helped. She bumped into something. It was a tight space, stuffy, hot. She reached up. Her hand didn't go far, touched metal. That bastard had her in a car trunk. He'd better let her out.

She didn't know when he'd moved her. She'd been on the back seat before, she was sure. Semi-conscious but she could tell the difference. It had been easier to move, easier to breathe.

She smacked the bottom of the trunk with an open hand. It stung, didn't do much else, not even a loud noise. The trunk hadn't budged. She wondered what would happen if she kicked it. Probably not much. She wriggled her toes, realized she was barefoot. She felt her mouth. She wasn't gagged. She didn't know what the deal was with air in a car trunk, how much she could exert herself without passing out. She could breathe, for now anyway. But how long? All the dicks she'd known, and this stranger was going to kill her.

She turned her head so she faced down, cleared her throat. Spit fell from her mouth to the mat of the trunk's floor cover, thin as a cheap motel carpet. It had been a while since she'd known one of those. She'd thought she left the cheapest things, the worst things, behind her.

Olivia rolled onto her back and screamed loud as she could. Loud in the trunk, anyway; she didn't know beyond that. She pulled her legs back so her knees were to her belly. Her legs hurt so bad she cried. She kicked as hard as her weakened legs allowed. The soles of her feet seemed to jar the bottom of the trunk a little.

"Help!" she yelled, as her legs landed in agony on the trunk's floor cover. Even more pain than before as she pulled her knees to her belly and lashed out with her feet once more, a little stronger this time.

"Help!" she yelled again, because why not as her legs dropped like they'd been struck down by an external force, not by their own pain and exhaustion. They hurt just lying flat on the trunk's mat. She yelled once more as she gathered the strength to again kick her only exit.

Her initial tears had stopped early in her exertions. They resumed now. She pulled her legs up and launched them once more. She gathered her breath—it took a minute this time—and yelled "Help!" to the world, knowing her world might not extend beyond the inside of this car trunk, knowing she'd keep kicking and yelling until she was saved or someone shut her up.

Vollmer waited in his car as the guy crossed to the house. Cobb. Fuckin' lackey, that's what Rico called him, guy who thought he was independent but needed Tenny for jobs that paid anything. Vollmer didn't know what lackey meant, maybe someone so dumb he parks a few car lengths ahead and doesn't notice the guy in the car behind him, just goes in. And leaves someone makin' a helluva noise in his trunk. Had to be that other broad, the one Rico visited while he met Theresa and the kid. Vollmer didn't know she was missing.

He watched Cobb cross the street, try to case the house from outside. He waited. It sucked about Stone, showing up at the other house when he did. Probably acted as amateur as Cobb was here, seeing nothing inside but never turning his head. He coulda told 'em both, go up real careful or you're dead.

Cobb was lucky no one heard that noise and checked

out his car trunk. Until now, as Vollmer got out and eased his car door shut behind him. He dropped his lit cigarette, opened his own trunk and put a flask of Jameson inside his jacket. He removed a steel pry bar and two thick blankets and left the trunk open. He looked across the street. Cobb had turned the corner between the house and garage, was out of sight.

Vollmer walked to the back of Cobb's car, dropped the blankets onto the street, knelt down on them and wedged the flat tip of the bar into a gap under the trunk lid. He pushed and pried. When it felt like it was in deep enough he stood and yanked upward. The lid creaked, popped open. Vollmer set the bar on the ground and lifted the trunk the rest of the way.

The girl lay there, not blindfolded and nothing stuffed in her mouth to shut her up—Cobb had the sense to know she could choke to death, not the sense to tape her mouth shut—and she was beat up bad.

"Quiet," he said, soft. She'd looked about to scream. "I'm gonna get you somewhere safe. But I gotta hide you first. From them." He looked across the street. No sign of Cobb yet.

He picked up the blankets, covered her with them, and lifted her.

She attempted a yell but not much volume.

"Quiet." His voice stayed soft, calming. She stopped. He carried her to the trunk of his own car, sat her down inside. She braced herself up, both hands behind her.

"One more ride inside like this. I'll make this ride nicer."

"No," she rasped. Her throat had to be dry.

"Don't lie down yet," he said. "Want a drink?"

Her head fell forward.

He took it as a nod, got the flask from his jacket, unscrewed the lid. "Tip your head back." He pressed the flask to her lips.

Olivia brought up a hand to grab it, fell sideways. Vollmer caught her shoulder, steadied her. "Keep your hand down. I'll hold the flask."

Her hand dropped and her head tipped back. Vollmer tipped the flask and she drank. He pulled the flask away.

"More," she said.

"Just a little," Vollmer said. "It's a short ride, but we ain't goin' yet."

She took another swig and Vollmer took his flask back.

"Now lie down," he said.

She must have heard that as an order; she did what she was told.

He lowered the lid gradually, shut it, grabbed his steel pry bar from behind Cobb's car and put it on the floor of his own car so it jutted out under the driver's seat. He locked his car and stood behind it, watched the house a few minutes. She was quiet. Good. Else he'd kill her.

All through this he'd kept an eye out for Cobb, hadn't seen him.

Waiting for an opening, a clear shot at the front door, Cobb heard something, peeked around the front corner of the house. A man was let in, no one came out. No window for those inside to watch from so he ran to the front of the house, his pistol under his coat. He slowed and walked up the steps to the front door. He wasn't about to knock and he couldn't stand outside for long. He'd get inside somehow. And kill every man in the house. Once he got what he needed from the woman and her kid, they wouldn't live either.

Platt glared at Willis. "We're in kitchens way too much. What'm I, a fuckin' cook?"

"The broad talks to Tré," Willis said. "We need you when that asshole Dust shows up."

"You sure the guy in the last house wasn't him?"

"Some other asshole," Willis said. "Don't worry. You're in charge of all the assholes."

"And you're in charge of me." Platt damn near growled the words.

"Take it up with Keene you don't like it."

Platt kept glaring.

Willis glared back.

Something slammed in the front of the house. Sounded like the door. Then a gunshot.

Platt moved fast into the living room as another gunshot blasted. He and Tré faced the front door as it creaked open.

A man stood there, blood streaming down one side of his face. He staggered forward and Platt opened fire.

The man fell forward.

A lean man in a black leather jacket stepped in behind him, two shots from his Glock .50 already fired at Platt's chest. As Platt fell the new man turned and fired two shots into Tré's chest before he could raise the pistol holstered on his hip.

The man with the Glock grabbed Theresa from the couch, stood her between him and the kitchen. "Someone else here?" he asked, swatting backward at Jeremy with his other hand, not hitting the boy but moving him away. He walked her forward.

"You," she said, recognizing Vollmer. "He was in there." She tipped her chin toward the kitchen.

A back door slammed shut. Vollmer kept walking her forward, keeping Theresa between him and the back of the house. No one in the kitchen, just a shut back door.

"Stop," Theresa said, and started to cry.

Vollmer made sure the back door was locked and walked her back to the living room.

Jeremy stood in front of the couch bawling, three dead men on the floor around him, the front door wide open.

"Let's go," Vollmer said. "Before someone shows up."

He walked the crying mother and child at gunpoint to his car, as fast as they'd move. "The kid in back," Vollmer said. "You ride shotgun. And calm the fuck down or you join the broad in the trunk."

Rico sat in Keene's office, cold coffee in the cups between them, nothing to say. Keene left the office a few times, always came back quickly. Problems that could be dealt with in a man's own home, or whatever the fuck this was.

Rico's phone buzzed. The display said Vollmer. Vollmer's phone anyway. Maybe he was dead and someone else had it. Rico picked up. "Yeah."

"Got some of your packages." Vollmer: to the point in as few words as possible. "Need a place to stay. Now."

"Where are ya?"

"Berkeley." He laughed. "Where the action is."

"Hang on." Rico lowered the phone, looked at

Keene. "It's my guy, the one I worried about. We gotta meet."

"He's alive?"

"And says he got packages."

"Lemme talk to him," Keene said.

Rico picked up his phone. "Talk to this guy," he said. "He's our host." He passed the phone to Keene.

Vollmer saw the guards outside the front door before he saw the address. Rico wouldn't set him up unless he'd fucked up, and the guys who fucked up were dead at that other house. He called Rico. "I'm here. Gonna need a hand with the packages. Best if I can unload in the garage."

It was only a minute before one guard stepped off the porch and over to the driveway. It was gated. The gate opened at someone's electronic command and the guard held a palm out to Vollmer like a traffic cop telling him to stop. The garage door opened and a Mercedes backed out carefully into the street then swung a sudden U-turn, pulled up behind where Vollmer was parked. The guard in the driveway waved Vollmer forward with a full arm sweep.

Vollmer pulled into the driveway and the Mercedes followed, the gate closing behind it. It was a two car garage, a classic Cadillac in one space. Vollmer didn't know cars but he knew when one looked valuable. He pulled in beside the Cadillac and parked as the garage door shut behind him.

Four men with pistols in their hands emerged from inside the garage. Two approached each side of the car. Vollmer spat out his open window as one neared his door. "Don't touch me." He opened the door, pushed the button that popped the trunk. "I got the merchandise."

One thug opened the front passenger door, another the back.

Vollmer stepped out, looked at the armed man in front of him. He kept his own pistol holstered, wrong place to pull it. "One in the trunk needs help getting out."

Beyond the front of Vollmer's car, on the left, a door looked like it led into the house. The man beside Vollmer waved him toward the door with his .45.

Vollmer shook his head. "Don't walk behind me. Next to me."

The man pulled his gun hand back and to the side, swung it at Vollmer's head. Vollmer ducked and came up beneath the man's underarms, held him aloft. The .45 grazed the side of Vollmer's head. He twisted the gunman's wrist and the pistol dropped, then he turned the man in mid-air so he looked at the other three armed men.

"No one shoots," Vollmer said, his forearm up at the held man's throat, and backed to the door, the held man flailing arms and legs. Vollmer reached up with one hand and yanked the head of the man he carried to one side. The man yelled in pain but stopped flailing, breathed fast through his mouth instead. Vollmer could've broke his neck. For now he just reached back, turned the doorknob and pushed it open. He dropped the man, let him fall as he backed into the house and pulled his Glock. "Bring 'em," he said, and got out his phone with his free hand.

He pressed Rico's speed dial number, talked as soon

as Rico answered. "Best get our host here before I kill all these dicks."

Keene's voice came through the open door. "Everyone lower their guns."

Vollmer glanced over his shoulder. Rico stood in front of Keene. Rico nodded.

Vollmer waited until Keene's guards lowered their guns, then lowered his. No one put his pistol away.

In the hall behind Keene, two more guards stood along each wall.

"Bring," Keene paused, "the packages first."

Theresa and Jeremy were walked in past Vollmer, then past Rico and Keene. The last guard followed, carrying Olivia.

Keene said to the last guard, "Take her to the living room couch. Stay with her. And the others. You two," he said to the guards guiding Theresa and Jeremy, "get them to the living room then back to your posts."

Keene gave them room then followed, turned when he reached his office. The door was open and he walked in. Rico followed, then Vollmer. The guards along the wall came last, shut the door behind them, took their usual positions in the office.

Keene sat, nodded at Rico and Vollmer to join him. They did. "Now," Keene said to Rico, "your man knows he answers when I ask, right?"

Rico looked at Vollmer. "He knows."

Keene turned to Vollmer. "What happened at the house?"

"Which house?"

"You know about both?"

"Was inside both." Vollmer shrugged. "First one, I'd a took 'em but they had it guarded. Pulled back, like I was supposed to." He smiled at Rico, like following orders was his reason. "Was across the street when Stone showed."

"Stone?" Rico looked surprised.

"He went round back." Vollmer's eyes were with Keene again. "Like I did. Only Stone don't come out. They left without him, two cars. One car with one guy, probably dumping evidence. I followed the other car."

Keene turned to Rico again. "Stone's one of yours."

"Yeah," Rico said, "was. Said he was comin', never said he was here."

"Gone now," Vollmer said. He'd known Stone for years. That's the way it goes. "They left, I followed. Was watchin' from my car when Cobb showed."

"Cobb?" Keene said.

"A rogue," Rico said. "Works for Tenny sometimes."

"Worked," Vollmer said. "Tried to take the second house. Through the front. Got shot. Through the front. And the back." Vollmer shrugged. "I went in behind him, took out two guys. Tall one got away."

"Two," Keene said, nodding. Good soldiers dead in this bullshit, not even the war. "You're costing me," he said to Rico. "I need that Tenny money now."

"Dust money," Rico said. "Get it from the bitches and the kid."

Keene smiled, more thoughtful than threatening this time. "This your man who's better than Platt?"

Rico kept his fucking mouth shut. A good man loves his family, takes pride in what they do. Rico didn't have family. He had Vollmer. He used to have Dust. Now he used one to find the other. Families don't always stay together.

Rico and Vollmer told Keene what they knew about Dust, some of it shit Keene knew already. Plus, what Dust had done recently—collecting for Tenny then ripping him off. The women and the kid were their only leads so far and they weren't talking.

Keene left them alone with the office guards and entered the living room.

Theresa and Jeremy sat close on one couch. Olivia looked mangled on the couch perpendicular to theirs. She lay almost flat yet bent, barely conscious.

A position of someone who'd suffered. Keene was familiar with it. "You know a lot about Dust." Her face was too pained to show surprise at the high pitch of his voice. "You need to say more. Everything."

"I…" Olivia's mouth barely opened. "Told them."

"I'm not them," Keene said. "They're not here. They got in someone's way. They're dead. Don't get in mine."

Olivia shuddered. Her whole body clenched. "What," she said, toneless. "Ask."

"Dust took money. It's mine. Where is it?"

"I. Don't know."

"Where's he?"

Her head shook one way, stopped on its way back. Tears came down. "He leaves. A woman for me. Then me for a woman. Find her. Or the next one."

Keene sat on the couch, below Olivia's bent knee, reached out softly, touched one cheek with a callous hand. "Maybe he thought you were the one. He told you a little. He told that bitch," Keene tipped his head toward Theresa, brought his eyes back to Olivia, "nothin'. Jack shit. What did he say, back when you were a beauty?"

"What," Olivia said, "do I look like now?"

Vanity. Keene loved it. Weakness talked. "You look like a woman some dead asshole beat the shit out of. Some other asshole beat you before that. Dust. He's the asshole I care about."

"He didn't talk to her!" Jeremy shouted from the other couch. "He talked to me!"

Keene turned with a horrible grin. Theresa held Jeremy tighter, like she could push his words back into him.

"He tell you where Dust might go?"

"Dust talked about what he does. What a man does, and all the jobs where you can break your nose. I don't think he ever broke his. Did you ever break yours?"

"Where'd he like to go?"

Jeremy looked at Theresa. "Do you know, mom?" He looked back at Keene. "I know he went away sometimes, that's all."

Keene's glare spread, took in both of them.

Theresa caught his eyes, answered. "Dust never said. Said it was safer for us if we didn't know."

Keene stepped toward her, squatted, put his face in hers. "Tell me now or you're both dead."

Theresa gulped. She'd been strong so long. Tears started like they'd never stop.

Keene turned to Olivia. "You too. Tell me where he might be or die."

"I," Olivia said, and stopped. "He never told me a goddamn thing."

Keene's eyes scanned across the three of them. They wouldn't know which place Dust actually went, but they had to know some place he'd mentioned. Places. There should be options. But Theresa cried, Olivia sat quiet, no one told him what he had to know.

His eyes took in each of them, made sure they looked back. "Someone gotta talk. Or you're all gonna die." Keene left the room.

Just victims and guards now.

Theresa stopped crying, held Jeremy tight. "They won't really kill us," she said. "They're just trying to scare us."

"Why do they want us scared?"

"They think we might know where Dust went."

"I know, but...do you think Uncle Dust will come save us?"

The idea was laughable. Theresa didn't even smile. "If he gets past his problems, he might. He had a lot of problems when he left...us."

On the other couch, Olivia lay quiet, her visible injuries augmented by a look on her face that didn't disagree. She didn't chime in, though. The three of them were in this together, but this might be the last chance for that woman to have a talk with her son.

Valerie considered. Valerie drank. Valerie drove.

She was headed to Oakland, no specific destination once she got there. With her disability payments, she could move in almost anywhere she applied. Not that her payments would get her into a ritzy area, but ritzy areas weren't anywhere she'd apply. She grew up on dirty streets, without money. Didn't trust the stuff. She was a fool not to head up here before. A place where an ass as huge as hers was a good thing.

So long as she was done with the Dust bullshit. Leave him behind along with the men who chased him. Go away from where he'd lived, into a dangerous neighborhood where she'd feel safer. She was going to spend what was left of her life having fun.

Carelli parked across the street. He knew this was the address, knew there was supposed to be a Volvo in the driveway. Almost always. It wasn't there now. Maybe she was out picking up her disability check, but he didn't like it. He waited for her to return, disliked it more every second.

He waited two hours. Called Rico: "Dust never went to Oakland. He's with the other broad. The one down south, I looked into it. She's gone, he's gone. Only way we find her, she puts in for her disability money. Monitor that, we know where she is. And then we know she ain't with him anymore. Him and all his money."

"My money," Rico said. "Don't forget my money. Or you want what you said? Your word's your life."

"I get him with more time," Carelli said.

"You got no more time," Rico said. "I get my money, or you got no time at all."

Rico put down the phone, his eyes on Keene. "The three out there ain't gonna tell us where Dust is. He's with another broad, on the run. The one down south. Valerie."

"You got a line on this bitch? How far south?"

"Near Monterey. Closer to my guys than yours."

Rico picked up his phone, made a call and gave the man who answered the address. "Read that back." He waited, nodded at the answer. "Right. I want everyone in the area on this. We don't care about the broad.

Don't matter what happens to her. She's with Dust. We need him. He can disappear, so long as we know where. That's number one. But we want the money too."

Rico put the phone down again.

Keene had his own phone in his hand. "You sure he's with her?"

"Got it from Carelli."

Keene grabbed a little notepad and a pen from the desk behind him, put them down in front of Rico. "Write down that address."

Rico wrote it down and Keene made a damn near identical phone call, looked at Rico when he was done. "Now what?"

"Those three." He tipped his head back to indicate whatever room the women and child were taken to. "We don't need 'em."

"They're your witnesses," Keene said. "You take care of 'em. Not here."

"One witness ain't here. And he's one of yours."

"You're right. He's one of mine," Keene said. "Means he ain't a witness. I'm talkin' the three here."

"We get these outta the neighborhood," Rico said, "what happens with your guy?"

"Willis knowin' shit is like you knowin' shit. He already knew more."

"But now," Rico said, "he knows shit about my people. And he ain't my people."

Keene shook his head. "You ain't gotta worry."

"No," Rico said. "I gotta fix. Only way this works— your guy's with Vollmer. They do the witnesses together."

"That slows down the hunt."

"I take slow over murder one any day of the week."

* * *

Keene called Willis. Within an hour, Willis was led into the office. Keene remained seated, Rico and Vollmer on either side of him. "Sit," Keene said.

One seat free and Willis took it. The fear and surprise on his face when he saw Vollmer were gone when he pulled his chair up.

"You've practically met Vollmer already," Keene said, and nodded at Vollmer. "This," he gestured to his left, "is Rico."

Rico looked, as usual, pissed off and dangerous, and Vollmer had killed Platt, one of the most efficiently murderous men Willis had known. Willis kept his face calm, nodded at each man. He didn't ask why he was here or anything else; this was Keene's party, he'd be told soon enough. Curiosity made a man look weak.

"We got a problem," Keene said, "in the other room. You and Vollmer gonna take care of it."

"What kinda problem?"

"You saw what happened at that house," Keene said. "So did they."

"I didn't see," Willis said. "I got an idea."

Vollmer glared at him. "You saw enough."

Willis avoided Vollmer's gaze, looked at Keene instead. "They the ones from the house? The ones we gotta take care of?"

"All three," Keene said.

"Three," Willis echoed. Two women and a kid. "And I'm part of this because?"

"Because you join the wolves," Keene said, "or they feed on you."

* * *

They're going to kill all of us, Olivia thought. But it won't do any good to say it. The mother and child— Theresa and Jeremy—would panic. There's no attacking the armed guards, no persuading the men in charge. But they didn't need to kill. Her and Theresa and Jeremy— they said it was crazy in that room, no one saw a thing. There was nothing to witness, just something that hit like a hurricane. The killings were a blur, and the dead men worked for the men who were now her captors. Despite the threats to kill, these men had to see that and do what made sense. They had to.

Willis drove, Theresa in the passenger seat beside him. Vollmer had lain Olivia's head in one corner of the backseat, her body angled so her legs stretched to the floor on the opposite side, where Vollmer sat. Between them Jeremy's shoulders were pulled together like there was even less room for him than there was. He looked almost as uncomfortable as Olivia, whose face showed, if anything besides pain and fear, the numbness of resignation. Jeremy's calves were pressed tight against the seat so he wouldn't touch her legs where they hung just beyond his.

On Vollmer's face, a smirk. "Where we goin'?" His pistol was holstered under his coat. He could get it out soon enough.

"East Oakland. A park I know."

"You the only one who knows it?"

"A lotta things get lost there," Willis said. "Don't get found fast."

"You're going to leave us in a park?" Olivia said. Theresa turned and glared at her. "Because, you know, that would give you time to get away. And what happened in that house was too fast, we never even saw it."

"Somethin' like that," Willis said. "That's enough talk."

"You don't like when the woman talks?" Vollmer asked. "She got a right to know what happens to her. She can't change anything."

"It won't help anything," Willis said, his eyes on the road.

"Maybe it's you," Vollmer said. "You don't wanna think about what you gotta do."

"We don't gotta talk about this now," Willis said.

"What else is there?" Vollmer got out a cigarette, lit it. "No ashtrays in the back seat?" He rolled down his window as they approached the freeway on-ramp.

Willis accelerated. The wind blew strong.

Vollmer rolled up his window. "You got somethin' for the ashes? Or I use the seat."

Willis looked around fast. Nothing to pass back. "Put it out the window."

"Ain't done yet," Vollmer said, and flicked ashes on the floor. "You control shit, don'tcha?"

"What are you talking about?"

"Usually you got a crew, you make the rules and they gotta follow, cuz you got Keene behind you." Vollmer laughed. "Keene about served you up this time."

Willis changed lanes, swerved around someone, changed back.

"You ain't gonna ask what I mean," Vollmer said.

"I know what you mean."

"Oh yeah," Vollmer said, "you're one a those smart

guys. Keep a guy around like that guy I shot, to keep the women and children quiet, you're in control. But I ain't like that stupid motherfucker. He's dead, and you're in the shit with me. Only I step outta shit all the time. You don't like to get your shoes dirty."

"What the fuck," Willis kept his speed steady at seventy in the second lane from the left, "are you talkin' about?"

"You're in this with me on these three. And you don't know if you can do that."

"What are you fuckin' sayin'?"

"You're scared," Vollmer said. "You think you're a boss, but you think Keene never did his own killin'? That fucker breathes murder. Rico too. They wish they could be in this car right now. Do it themselves instead a count on someone else. But Rico knows he can count on me."

"Stop!" Theresa shouted, facing Vollmer. "Shut up about this! I have a boy in this car!"

Vollmer gave Theresa a full-toothed smile, spoke soft. "Fuck you, bitch."

"She's right," Willis said. "You talk too much."

"I'm not here to make you happy," Vollmer said. "I don't make people happy. Except my bosses. I say what I fucking want, all a you can shut up. Shit, no one here's gonna breathe a word."

"We're not gonna talk," Olivia said. "That's all you mean, right?"

Vollmer laughed, shook his head. "You ain't exactly a threat."

"You talk like you're killin' us anyway."

"Maybe I do." Vollmer turned away from her. "How far?" he asked Willis.

"Off the freeway soon," Willis said. "Then just a couple miles."

Jeremy sat quiet between Vollmer and Olivia, ignored until now. Vollmer patted him on the shoulder. "You and your mom get shy?"

"I don't like how you talk to her."

"Your Uncle Dust taught you how a man lives, right? Does a man let people tell him to shut up? Does a man worry about what scares other people? Or does he just do what needs getting done?"

"A man takes charge," Jeremy said, slowly, like he knew the questions were a trap.

"And you're gonna be a man," Vollmer said. "You're gonna talk when there's talkin' to be done."

"What do you want to talk about?" Jeremy asked.

"Life," Vollmer said, smiling, "and how you talk about Dust or you got no more of it."

"Uncle Dust is great," Jeremy said. "He taught me how to fight. But sometimes he's an asshole. He says so. Mom says it's because he drinks."

"Assholes are assholes," Vollmer said. "Some of 'em drink. What do you know about Dust?"

"He's a good fighter. And he had a job telling people why they should pay what they owed. And he cares about me and my mom. You better not hurt us."

"We seen how much he cares about people," Vollmer said. "And he's the reason this bitch," Vollmer tipped his chin toward Olivia, "got that scar across her face. Dust stole money. The way he did it, he left you to die. You got somethin' helps me find the money?"

Theresa glared at Vollmer. "Leave him alone!"

"He's alone," Vollmer said. "You too."

"He's a boy," she said.

"His age," Vollmer said, "I was on the street. If I was a boy, I'd be dead."

"You were a boy," Theresa said. "Even if you pretended you weren't."

Vollmer pulled his Glock from the holster under his jacket. "Everyone shut up."

They were still on the freeway, everyone's windows up. Vollmer's cigarette had dropped ashes all across the floor and on his shoes. "Except you, Willis."

"You always gotta say my name?"

"If it matters, I don't say it." Vollmer smoked. "It don't matter."

Willis coughed. "Could you roll down your goddamn window?"

"Not on the freeway. It's cold. Not off the freeway, cuz they could scream out the window."

Willis sighed. "Why should I talk?"

Vollmer blew more smoke. "You wanna change my mind."

"About what?"

"To me," Vollmer said, "you're just a victim who has to do this thing or die. Fuck, I could give a pistol to the kid, maybe he's one of us. I know you ain't. No matter what you do."

Willis moved a lane to the right, negotiated traffic and got over two more lanes then to the off-ramp.

"We do this at rush hour," Vollmer said, "so you could show off your driving?"

Willis took a left off the freeway then cut between cars and took the first right, off the busy main road to an also crowded back street, a row of cars waiting for their turn at the stop sign. "You're welcome."

"Yeah, well, this part of the strategy ain't so impressive."

"We don't stay on this street either, fuckhead. Two blocks of this then a left and we head up the hill. There's a park up there, no idea what its name is. Know what it's called, though. The Shroud. A lovely place at night."

Willis took the route he said he would. The hill was slow, a lot of curves. Ten minutes without another car on the road. He pulled over.

"Fuckin' dark up here," Vollmer said, sounding pleased.

They stepped away from the car, pistols at the backs of the child and two women ahead of them.

Fifty feet away, Willis said, but it was dark and there were trees and tall brush; they couldn't see far ahead, they walked damn slow. Especially Olivia. She struggled all the way, bent forward for breath a couple times.

"Stop here," Willis finally said, after what had to have been a hundred feet.

The captives stood at the far edge of a short stretch of dirt, just short of where the grass resumed.

"Here?" Vollmer said. The grass grew two feet high just beyond where they'd stopped. "You done this before?"

"I know what I'm doing," Willis said.

"And I know what you should be doing." Vollmer addressed the three in front of them. "Step into the grass."

"Mommy," Jeremy said, sounding younger than he was. He stepped into the grass, Theresa with him.

Olivia took a step and dropped to the dirt, the grass in front of her.

Vollmer spat next to where she landed. "Crawl if you gotta."

Theresa and Jeremy looked back at Olivia. She dragged herself forward. Jeremy shook his head back and forth and cried. Theresa put an arm around his shoulders, pulled him tight. Her own tears dripped.

Olivia also began to cry, but she reached out with one hand, pulled herself forward. Still short of the grass, she turned her head, faced Vollmer and Willis.

"Please," she said. "I'll ball both of you." Her pout was far from sexy, her face filled with fear.

"The way you look," Vollmer said, "it'd feel like rape. Keep crawlin'."

Theresa and Jeremy watched as Olivia dragged herself forward.

Olivia blinked her wet eyes at Vollmer. "And you don't rape."

"No."

"But you kill."

"Some shit's mercy. Some shit can't be. Get in the grass."

Olivia stayed on the edge of the grass and the dirt. She screamed.

Vollmer raised a foot high and kicked her in the back, knocking her forward. "In the grass! On your knees! All of you!"

They all got on their knees, Olivia screaming, Jeremy crying, Theresa whispering, "It'll be okay, we'll be okay, it'll be okay, we'll be okay."

"Now lie down." Vollmer turned to Willis, talked soft. "Get out your pistol, we shoot together, one to the head, each of 'em, left to right. On the count of three."

Olivia let out a new scream and the others joined her.

Willis pulled his pistol, the look in his eyes one Vollmer had seen in men who knew they were about to die.

The child and women kept screaming.

Vollmer counted, a steady beat. "One." The screams got higher. "Two." Higher still. "Three." And higher.

Willis hesitated and Vollmer glared at him. Willis fired, shot Olivia in the back of the head, then Jeremy, then Theresa.

Vollmer waited until Willis had shot them all, grinned at him, raised his Glock and blasted each victim once more. "You shoot shitty, mighta only gave 'em brain damage. Not now. Murder one for both of us. You stand tall with that?"

They lay dead. Two women and a child.

Business is business.

Willis looked calm. "Fine. Let's get outta here."

Vollmer would never fuck Theresa now. Too bad. And Olivia...Before Cobb got to her, Rico said she was hot. Was. Neither of them was Yula. If one of them was, and she wasn't a fucked up junkie, it wouldn't be Willis he left The Shroud with.

The drive back to Keene's place was silent.

Vollmer and Willis were led back to Keene's office. They took seats across the table from Keene and Rico. No guards in the room.

"How'd it go?" Keene asked.

"Job was fine," Vollmer said. "This guy shook and sweated the whole way back."

"Bullshit," Willis said.

"No one talked," Keene said, his eyes on Willis.

"No," Willis said.

"We ain't tossed the pieces yet," Vollmer said.

"What?" Rico sat up straighter.

"Never pulled over, still got 'em on us." He glanced at Willis. "I guess he figures they're only guns."

Keene stood, leaned across the table, grabbed Willis by the shirt and stood him up. "Get the fuck outta here with that shit!"

Willis stepped back, shook a second, straightened. He nodded at Keene and turned toward the door. Vollmer shoved his chair back and followed. Willis opened the door and they walked out. Vollmer pushed it shut.

Keene pushed his thin hair back and sat. "Jesus. In my house."

Rico nodded. "Woulda been in a river or the gutter if Vollmer drove."

"But he let Willis bring it back here."

"Wanted you to know," Rico said.

"He don't like Willis?" Keene said. "Fine. Don't need to bring it here."

"He let you know," Rico said. "That shit about your guys better than mine? Yeah. Can I get a drink here?"

"Yeah, yeah." Keene stood, got the Yamazaki from his desk, poured them each a few fingers. "Hardest part of the job—worryin' about my guys."

"When you ain't in a war," Rico said, "you let 'em die. Keep the good ones. Worry a lot less."

"Great," Keene said. "Talk about what I'm in, tell me what to do when I'm out. Thanks a lot, Rico."

"Kinda guy I am," Rico said.

They drank.

"Another thing," Keene said.

"Yeah?"

"I'm down two men 'cause of this bullshit. And I didn't get any of that Dust money to make it up. And I'm in a war. You gotta give me reasons not to kill you."

WITH THE RIGHT ENEMIES

"Money's easy," Rico said. "Carelli has ten large. I was supposed to get Dust for it. I can make that yours."

"Don't make up for two men," Keene said.

"And you're in a war. I know. Whadda you want?"

"Vollmer. And one more guy. As long as this war lasts, they're mine. About a year, I think, maybe less. But they're mine 'til the war's over. Even if it lasts forever."

"I need Vollmer," Rico said.

"I ain't askin' fuckin' questions here. I get Vollmer, long as I need him, and I get the ten large and one more guy. Call Carelli. I want my money now."

Rico got his phone out, put in Carelli's number.

Carelli picked up. "Yeah?"

"Get back here. Now."

"On my way. Any news since what I gave you?"

"Yeah," Rico said. "News is, I'm with Keene and this game's over. Bring my money. It's his now. And don't forget what you said about your word."

Dust sat alone at a table against the wall, faced the door. The Crib wasn't his kind of place, a bunch of lower class rednecks or whatever you called them in the Midwest, but he couldn't go to his kind of place, might see someone who knew him. He just hoped no one pissed him off in here, he might kill the bastard. And there was no way he was dying in this place.

Like the choice of where he died was his. Only if he got suicidal. He wasn't that desperate. Tenny wanted him dead, Rico would too. Two men used to getting what they wanted. With Rico it wouldn't just be business, he'd think it was personal. Same as everyone Dust left

behind would take it personal, wouldn't see it as something he just had to do. But it was money and he was a
man who took money. Sometimes that meant leaving
people behind, whatever he thought of them.

Theresa wouldn't see that, Olive wouldn't either.
And he'd already heard what Val thought. She was
wrong, they were all wrong, but they were women, they
always wound up wrong about him. Jeremy, though: he
didn't know about kids, what happened when they
learned about the world. A different education than
what the boy got in school, that's for sure. It'd do him
good in the long run. Now? Jeremy might hate him,
might want to be like him. Nothing Dust could control.
Not his responsibility anyway.

Rico was the only one who could understand, but he
wouldn't. A good guy but a follower, mixed up things a
man had to do with things he did for his job, like serv-
ing a master was part of freedom. A practical thing,
maybe. Not like Rico was ever taking over from Tenny,
just his highest-ranking waterboy.

Any job with a boss was like that. Or too much time
with a woman. Always had to please someone else. Taking care of yourself was never enough.

The advantages of robbing banks. No bosses, no
rules, no sharing the money, just don't get caught. Especially now. Prison would be death for him, Tenny would
make sure of that.

He waved to Tina, the waitress, a busty thing in her
forties with a truckload of mascara and cigarette breath.
Her skin wasn't too bad. He pointed at each glass in
front of him. "Another. And don't end your shift without saying goodnight."

Her smile showed teeth fairly close to white. "Right

back, hon."

He supposed the regulars didn't tip much. It was days since he got laid, he didn't know how many. Tina was no prize but she had enough shape left to her, they could grab a bottle and go back to her place. Not to his, the hotel was too nice. Even with most of his cash in their safe, he didn't want strangers finding out how well he lived and where he stayed.

He had to learn some banks around here, get back to work. Nothing that would call attention to himself. God knows how widespread Tenny's bounty went. Anyone recognized him, he was dead, he was sure of that.

Robbing banks or dead, it was better than what he'd had. God damn those people who thought he betrayed them. God damn them for loving him.

His drinks arrived and he downed the shot, watched his date for later walk away. Nice walk. He sat tall and alert, drank his beer slow and enjoyed it, shut out the sounds of whatever the fuck music they were playing on the jukebox. He'd get as close to love as he needed tonight and be out of town tomorrow, covering less miles than the last couple days. Now that he'd put some distance between himself and Tenny he'd scout for banks as he traveled.

He finished his beer. Tina was across the room. He had to take a leak anyway. He stood, walked toward the toilets. He'd had a few but he could drink a lot, walked steady, saw Tina with her head turned a little so she could see him. He blew her a kiss. She grinned big, her cheeks pink. Dust headed to the can.

He pushed the men's room door with one hand. It was heavy, opened easy. He walked in, looked back at the two wide, pale men who came in behind him. Looked like they should hold pitchforks.

"You like Tina?" the first one said. He was six foot, maybe thirty, his short curly blond hair receding. He bulged through his large T-shirt in all directions. His friend, built the same but dark haired, stepped beside him.

Dust looked at the blond. "I wanna take a piss." He turned his head toward the urinals, turned back fast, bent low and threw a right uppercut to the blond's gut. The blond stepped back, gasped for breath.

Dust pivoted, stood tall as the dark haired man stepped back a second before wading in. That second was a mistake. Dust caught him in stride with a kick to the nuts and the second man buckled to his knees. Dust grabbed his hair and brought his head down as Dust's knee came up, smashed the nose and drove into the forehead. The man fell to the bathroom floor.

Dust straightened and stepped toward the blond again. The blond covered up in a boxer's stance, tossed a jab that wouldn't have hurt if it landed. Dust stepped into the blond, chest to chest, put both hands on his head and twisted hard in one direction. He let go and the blond dropped. If he was lucky it just hurt like hell, wasn't a broken neck. Either way, Dust had to get the fuck out of here.

He walked out of the men's room fast, kept going out of the bar and ran to his car. He'd drive the speed limit straight to his hotel, get his money and his shit and clear out. Looked like he wasn't getting laid tonight.

Vollmer drove home. They didn't find Dust so he'd killed five people for no extra money, whole trip was a waste. No fucking in it either. And he was tired, with nothing to do when he got home. He'd come back up and kill Willis at some point, but if he did it now he'd get blamed, would spend the rest of his life running like Dust.

Sometimes he preferred killing to fucking, but that was never the choice. A lot of times the choice was kill or die. Once in a while that choice involved women. Whoever it was, he'd always choose kill. And even though they'd shot the same people, Willis would plead him out if it came to that. Willis might not have considered that possibility. Keene probably had. So long as Willis was only warned and not guarded, it wouldn't be enough.

His phone rang. It sat on the passenger seat beside him. A number, no name. Probably a wrong number or a sales call, no one that mattered. He didn't bother picking up. Hardly anyone had his number. He liked it better that way.

He was making good time on 880, would hit traffic at Hayward of course, and maybe the edge of San Jose. If he was too awake when he got close to home he'd hit the whore streets, pass some time with another woman who wasn't Yula. Like the dead broads.

Rico got home, called an afternoon meeting with Vollmer. Lunch in a deli: he met with his collectors in the morning.

Rico showed up early to eat, had coffee and a massive corned beef on rye. Vollmer came through the door on time and Rico waved.

Vollmer sat across from him. It was only hours since Oakland. He didn't need coffee, didn't need food, just needed Rico to say why they were here.

Rico was chewing when Vollmer sat. Most of the sandwich remained; he'd get back to it. "You got no problems with our trip, right?"

Vollmer shook his head. "Only problem, we didn't find him. Cuts into my payday."

"But you're okay with that other part."

"I seen what happens when children live. How's the sandwiches here?"

"Best deli in town," Rico said. "You want somethin'? Order at the counter."

"Not now," Vollmer said. "You got work for me?"

"Nah." Rico took a drink of his coffee. "Just checkin' on ya."

"You never gotta worry about me," Vollmer said. "I can live with what I do. I already live with what I done."

"Yeah." Rico's teeth tore a piece of sandwich into his mouth and he chewed, swallowed. "There's a thing you need to do, though. Pack."

"Pack what?"

"Whatever you got," Rico said. "We owe Keene for the guys he lost. Go up there, work for him 'til this business is settled, maybe a year."

"A year?" Vollmer thought about being near Willis in a street war for a year. People on all sides were bound to die.

He smiled. "Yeah," he said. "Alright."

Rob Pierce wrote the novels *Uncle Dust* and *With the Right Enemies*, the novella *Vern in the Heat*, and the short story collection *The Things I Love Will Kill Me Yet*. Former Editor-in-Chief of *Swill Magazine* and co-editor at *Flash Fiction Offensive*, Rob has also edited dozens of novels for All Due Respect and freelance, and has had stories published in numerous ugly magazines. He is equally comfortable taking romantic walks on the beach or dumping the body elsewhere.

BOOKS

On the following pages are a few
more great titles from the
Down & Out Books publishing family.

For a complete list of books and to
sign up for our newsletter,
go to DownAndOutBooks.com.

Dirty Who?
A Johnny O'Rorke Novel
Jerry Kennealy

Down & Out Books
July 2018
978-1-946502-64-3

San Francisco Police Inspector Johnny O'Rorke, assisted by
Cosmo the Wonder Dog, a Lakeland terrier, get tangled up
in the search for a sadistic serial killer and along the way
brush up against the likes of Frank Sinatra, LSD guru Timothy O'Leary, a porno movie star by the name of Pierre
LaTongue and get involved in a deadly game of Irish Roulette.

Jerry Kennealy was the recipient of the 2017 Life Achievement Award by the Private Eye Writers of America.

Down on the Street
Alec Cizak

ABC Group Documentation,
an imprint of Down & Out Books
978-1-943402-88-5

What price can you put on a human life?

Times are tough. Cabbie Lester Banks can't pay his bills.
His gorgeous young neighbor, Chelsea, is also one step
from the streets. Lester makes a sordid business deal
with her. Things turn out worse than he could ever have
imagined.

Vern in the Heat
A Crime Novella
Rob Pierce

All Due Respect, an imprint of
Down & Out Books
April 2018
978-1-948235-22-8

Vern is a dangerous man—he makes illegal exchanges safe. Until someone tries to rip off a drug deal he's working and he gets blamed.

Now both gangs involved are after him, including the one he works for. And he's going to clear his name, no matter who he has to kill in the process.

Fast Bang Booze
Lawrence Maddox

Shotgun Honey, an imprint of
Down & Out Books
978-1-946502-54-4

After seeing Frank deliver an impressive ass kicking in a
bar fight, Russian mobster Popov hires him to be his driver. What Popov doesn't know is that when Frank is sober,
he's inhumanly fast, deadly, and mute; when Frank is on
the sauce, he's a useless twenty-something wiseass.

Double-crossed in a drug deal gone bad, Frank and Popov
have one night to recover their stolen cash or get wiped off
the map. Frank's special abilities put him in the spotlight,
and he struggles to keep it all together...

CPSIA information can be obtained
at www.ICGtesting.com
Printed in the USA
LVHW032153221118
597954LV00002B/491/P